# FOR THE HOLIDAYS

A GAMING THE SYSTEM NOVEL

Brenna Aubrey

SILVER GRIFFON ASSOCIATES
ORANGE, CA, USA

Book Layout ©2020 BookDesignTemplates.com
Cover Art ©2020 Sarah Hansen, Okay Creations
Cover photo © Lindee Robinson Photography
Cover Models: Elena Filip and Marcus Filip

For The Holidays / Brenna Aubrey. – 1st ed.
ISBN 978-1-940951-78-2

www.BrennaAubrey.com

*For a dear & longtime friend, Sabrina. You virtually held my hand all through writing At Any Price and are still there now.*

*"A good friend is like a four leaf clover: hard to find and lucky to have." -- Irish Proverb*

# ACKNOWLEDGEMENTS

A book is never created in a vacuum and mine typically involve a lot of moving parts. And during an exceptionally difficult and trying year for us all, I'm extremely grateful for all who played a part in the making of this one.

So much gratitude for my intrepid and amazing first readers, Kate McKinley & Sabrina Darby, who never complained once when I sent them the very early and ugly first draft, read it, laughed and encouraged me even through all the typos, mistakes and gaps in the story. You push me constantly to make it a better book and you do it so well. I love you ladies!  Much thanks to Dayna Hart, a new addition to the team who helped me smooth over the finish product. For the gorgeous cover: Sarah Hansen of Okay Creations, Lindee Robinson of Lindee Robinson Photography and the real couple "stand-ins" for Adam & Mia : Marcus and Elena Filip.

For the Brenna Aubrey book group and the readers who give me life. I'm so amazed by this supportive group of people who look out for each other and stay connected via their love of my books. Thank you for sharing the laughs and the tears and for just being you. Much love to Kelly Allenby--for so much that if I had to list it, I'd need to write a whole other acknowledgements section--running the reader group, reaching out to readers and audiobook listeners, stepping in when I'm too absent-minded or overwhelmed to handle social media, etc. etc.  And thank you to early ARC readers for their early deep dives into the material. You're amazing and I love you. For all the loyal Gaming The System readers who've been here since At Any Price and are so invested in these fictional people who walk around in my head: you make it possible for me to be able to continue writing about them and I couldn't do it without you. I hope their continuing story is everything you've hoped for.

For my family... husband, the no-longer-so-little kiddos, I know you put up with a lot, particularly Mom disappearing for long periods of time while she's crashing toward deadline. I guess as teenagers, that isn't such a huge sacrifice anymore LOL. For Mom, my tireless encouragement and unconditional love--it means so much. Love you.

I've had many jobs during my adult life and this one has been a helluva ride. It's by far not the easiest, but definitely the best.

# CHAPTER 1
## *MIA*

WHY IS IT THAT WE MAKE PLANS FOR VACATION—TO spend a week of relaxation and escape—and in the process, we end up stressing ourselves to the brink to prepare for it? That's what this day had been for me—a thin slice in the middle of the stress sandwich that was my preparations for the holidays and the start of a new rotation in medical school.

Adam and I had just returned from my mom's place in Anza on Christmas night, having spent a few days with my mom and her husband, Adam's uncle Peter. In addition, we'd had Peter's kids, William and Britt, their significant others, and the grandkids.

Mom had planned an amazing little down home family Christmas for us all. We'd had some adventures—exploring and hiking, a little horseback riding with the kids, and playing a lot of crazy board games.

I sighed, adjusting a shimmery silver, star-shaped ornament on our gorgeous tree that stood nearly ten feet tall in our front room, and was still dwarfed by the cathedral ceilings. It was close to midnight on Christmas night, and I couldn't help but take a moment to admire the play of light and shimmery beauty in that quiet room. The colorful ornaments reflected the white lights, the shining red and gold ribbon against the soft green fir of the tree. Closing my eyes, I inhaled that fresh, clean scent that immediately took me back to hiking through Idyllwild forests as a kid.

Suddenly, strong, solid arms encircled my waist and pulled me back against a broad, hard chest. The tree's aroma was replaced by the familiar scent of the man I loved. Eyes still closed, I relaxed against him as he dipped his head to land a peck on my neck. A little thrill buzzed there, as it always did when he touched me. He rested his head against mine, and my eyes opened.

He was staring at the tree, all the glistening lights reflecting in his gorgeous dark eyes. "Crazy, we've barely had a chance to sit and just admire our tree. Here we are, no sooner home but headed back out of town."

I sighed. "The price we pay for being young and driven, I guess? Thank goodness for the holidays. It seems to be the only thing that can slow us down. I've been able to hog you mostly to myself for the past forty-eight hours."

"Only forces beyond our control can slow down people like us."

I swallowed, considering that. Before Christmas, we'd hardly seen each other, for nearly a month. He'd had a business trip. I'd had final exams. He'd spent nearly a week working with his charity foundation on end-of-year business items for the season… The list never ended.

I turned and landed a return peck on his whisker-rough cheek. "Maybe people like us should learn to slow down more often and savor what we have."

Adam smiled and his arms tightened around me. "Hey, it was your idea to go spend the week, and our first anniversary, up in the mountains with our friends."

"Mmm, true. We never get to see *them* anymore either. But we'll get our time alone. And now that you've promised to keep your phone locked in the safe while we're there, I'll actually get to have a real conversation with you that isn't rudely interrupted by beeping and buzzing."

"Yes, yes. Just pay no attention to all the twitching and withdrawal symptoms I'll be enduring in the process."

He joked now, but it had been a brief point of contention between us at first. He'd happily relented when I'd agreed not to bury my nose in my textbooks. Compromise was good and healthy and yet... I couldn't help but be a little worried about us. Even if it was just a tiny inkling of disquiet with no tangible basis.

We went to bed at the same time that night, something we almost never did normally. Sometimes we'd spend time together doing other things—watching TV, cuddling, sexy times. But Adam was rarely the type of guy who just rolled over and went to sleep afterward. He popped out of bed and was raring to go for a few more hours still.

The trying times of being married to a man who rarely got more than five hours sleep a night. As I waited for him to come to bed, I dawdled on my tablet, still distracted by some of those distant worries.

As luck would have it, the link for one of those silly internet quizzes crossed my feed and I, like an idiot, clicked on it. As if it were some kind of fortune teller that might set us straight, or even just calm some distant fears.

When Adam came to bed minutes later, slipping under the sheets, I was just answering the last question of the their "Rate Your Marriage" quiz on BuzzTea.

"What's so funny?" he asked, settling in beside me.

"Oh I followed some dumbass clickbait." I laughed. No need to alarm him that I'd actually gone looking for it. It was meaningless, anyway. I showed him the screen on my tablet. "I just took this quiz, and apparently we scored abysmally. BuzzTea gives us less than three years until divorce."

Adam didn't answer for a long moment—he seemed to be mulling it over. Then suddenly, as if what I'd said had finally sunk in, he stiffened, struggling to sit up. "What?! Let me see that."

"Don't get your blood pressure up. It's just a stupid internet quiz."

But Adam had already clicked on the retake button and was now sitting up in bed, spooning forgotten. He furiously drilled through the questions, every muscle in his body growing tenser and more upright with each passing question. I swallowed. "Adam, put it aside. It's something some intern on a deadline wrote while Googling shit. It's not—"

"*No.* No one's allowed to give us a low score. We don't roll like that." And with a flourish, he hit "see your results" and held his breath. "Shitty programming. I could do this way better, so it would give immediate results."

I nodded. "Of course you could."

"Listen, I'll go do it right now and it won't even take an hour to—Ah! here it is. See, that's a...." His voice faded as he squinted, scrutinizing the screen. The tablet illuminated his breathlessly handsome features. I never tired of looking at him, really. Okay, maybe sometimes when he was getting on my nerves. But lately we hadn't seen enough of each other for that to even happen.

Sadly, he really seemed to be taking this dumb quiz thing hard. Clearly, he needed a distraction. "Come here. That thing's bullshit." I bent and kissed his temple, his cheek, his neck, and I gripped the edge of the tablet, ready to whisk it away from his scrutiny. "They give us absolutely no points for burning up the bed when we have sex."

"Hmm," he said, apparently not hearing me as he clicked more links and, maddeningly, tried to take the thing again. I yanked it away and set it on my side of the bed, out of his reach.

He let it go, falling back against the pillow and looking at me. "It's complete BS," I repeated.

He shrugged. "I'm exhausted, anyway. I think I need a vacation to recuperate from Christmas. But I'll do it after I write the makers of that quiz a sternly worded letter of complaint."

I laughed. "You are such a nerd. But... you are *my* sexy, hot nerd."

He leaned in and kissed me. Now we were talking. I locked my arms around his neck just as he pulled back. "You realize we have to be up in four hours?"

I took in a deep breath and let it out. "Fair point. But once we're officially on our vacation, I expect all the sexy sex we can get."

"With seven of our closest friends in the same house."

I bit my lip. "Maybe inviting everyone up with us was a crazy idea?"

He kissed me again. "Let's have the most fun we've ever had on vacation."

"It's a deal."

Thankfully, as I rolled onto my side to fall asleep, he scooted back into spooning position. My lids closed, and dreamy almost-sleep grasped at me like the incoming tide lapped the dry sand.

Tonight, we were exhausted. It had been a wonderful Christmas, but tomorrow, we'd be in the snowy mountains doing fun things. I'd have him all to myself—and sometimes with friends—for a whole week. Then, the special surprise I'd planned for our very first wedding anniversary.

Things would be brighter. We'd reconnect and those thought gremlins would be banished once and for all.

I couldn't wait.

# CHAPTER 2
## *ADAM*

EMILIA THOUGHT I'D DROPPED IT.

As far as she was concerned, I had.

But that quiz was absolute bullshit. And I was on a mission to prove it. As we rode in the car to the airport to catch our three-hour flight to Vancouver, Canada, I was determined to design my plan of attack.

The goal? To prove that a low score on some stupid BuzzTea quiz meant nothing and that we, Emilia and I, as a married couple of 358 days, were not only amazing, but *goals*.

So suck it, BuzzTea. It was on.

I spent much of the travel time researching, making lists, and brainstorming ideas. What were the qualities of a successful marriage? Beyond just the answers to the questions that would score us higher on that one quiz, I wanted to know. Because it was important, damn it.

I was the best at everything I did. And this would be no different.

During my research phase, I took several more quizzes. Let's just say these people didn't know shit about Emilia and me and our marriage. We were busy these days, yes, and had to carve out time to see each other. I traveled, and she was in a very challenging medical school program which required many hours of study and working rotations.

So time wasn't on our side, and maybe lately we didn't have sex as much as they required—or rather, *recommended.* You had to be in the same time zone and zip code for that to happen, and in recent months, that hadn't been us.

And I didn't do phone sex. Which, I might add, is not sex at all. It's just getting yourself off with an audience.

My eyes skimmed the results of the fifth questionnaire. Maybe with all our no spare time we were forgetting to hold hands as much as we once did—or supposedly *should.* Had we ever been hand holders, much? It was hard to hold hands while playing video games.

Not that we did much of that together, either, anymore.

I frowned.

Maybe that damn article had a point? Maybe we were in trouble?

My heart raced at the thought, and I turned to look at my new wife as she dozed beside the window on the airplane. We were in the front row of first class and she'd tucked her long legs under her, her hands pressed palms together and she rested her head on them like a pillow. She must have been exhausted.

Even so, she was so beautiful. Even dressed in her comfy traveling clothes with minimal makeup. Or anytime, really. I brushed a stray strand of hair out of her face and her long eyelashes fluttered open.

I took advantage, shoving my shoulder as far over as I could. "Here, nap on my shoulder."

"Mmm," she mumbled and obediently pushed forward to rest her head on my shoulder. It took a few tries to get comfortable.

She reminded me of a finicky cat finding just the right spot to lie down in, but eventually she found it. The minute she did, I turned to smell her hair and give her a light kiss on the top of her head.

Then, I went back to work accumulating all the data I needed to make our marriage the top of the marriage leaderboard. We'd *pwn* all the rest.

I took another long sniff of her hair, the rush of love hitting me like a drug. Mmm. Yeah, it was like the hit directly to my blood. Of course, now I was reminded of how long it had been—over a week now—since we'd had sex. Our lives had been *that* crazy busy.

As she'd said, we were going to be spending time together. I'd make it all about catching up on lost time and opportunities.

I couldn't wait.

But I couldn't put that goddamn quiz out of my mind. So as she slept on my shoulder on the short flight northward, I seethed, and I planned.

I wouldn't have my phone for much longer to help with the research. I'd promised Emilia I'd lock it away for a week. My staff had been given instructions to reach out to her and Jordan in case of an emergency.

She did have a point. When I had my phone in hand, it often came between the two of us enjoying our time together. We control-freaks rolled like that. But I'd done this before, for shorter periods of time, and I was ready.

I was going to pour all of my energies into us and upping our score. I made my list of all the ways we were going to correct course and kick marriage quiz ass.

None of that "finished in three years" bullshit. Nope. We were going to grow old together. And that was that.

*** 

Two big SUVs picked us up at the airport and carted all nine of us into the mountains toward the world-renowned resort of Whistler and the mansion we'd reserved for our getaway week.

A smiling concierge greeted us along with a blast of cold air that, if I'd felt sleepy before, completely woke me up. Snow was on the ground everywhere, and a gorgeous backdrop of mountains cut a jagged edge in the horizon. The concierge, Anna, informed us that fresh snow was predicted for practically every day of our stay.

The women in our group all waxed poetical on the luxurious cozy interior and the magnificent views. Jordan, Heath and Lucas were very impressed by the fully stocked bar and a billiards table just adjacent. Within minutes, Kat ferreted out the console in the den and I cursed myself that I hadn't forbidden video games while we were here. That'd be about as easy as soloing a boss mob at a high-end raid, though. We were mostly a group of gamers, after all.

Maybe I'd make it a rule for just Emilia and me. I had to admit to more than a little thrill at putting my complete focus on her.

Also on making her moan with pleasure and saying my name as many times as possible in that deep, throaty voice. Yes, I'd definitely added that to my list. At the top, bottom, and in the middle.

And speaking of my list… I made sure, before my lovely wife confiscated my phone to lock away, that I found the nearest conveniently-placed pad of hotel stationary to scratch down my notes—in the form of a bullet-point action plan—to keep handy.

By the time this week was through, we were so going to be on the marriage leaderboard.

Eat shit, BuzzTea.

# CHAPTER 3
## *JORDAN*

T HIS MORNING, I'D STEPPED OFF THAT PLANE, SMUG AS fuck with a secret in my pocket. A three-point-five carat secret, to be exact.

Yeah, I was taking a massive risk carrying this thing around in my jacket pocket. The girlfriend, she wasn't a slouch when it came to ferreting out a secret. Hell, she'd flushed out all my deepest, darkest secrets long ago, and hopefully had moved on to new hunting grounds. Because I had a big one right now, one that she wouldn't discover, if all went well, until just the perfect time.

Only problem was that I had yet to discover what, exactly, was the perfect time for it.

After passing through customs in Squamish and making our way to the private cars that would drive us to the mansion in Blackcomb, near Whistler, we were greeted by our concierge and her assistant who were waiting with hot towels and, inside, a tray full of champagne.

As they rattled off a carefully prepared welcome speech of things they'd planned for us, I considered carefully my next steps. The concierge looked like a glammed-up snow-bunny, all dressed in pale pink and fluffy wool. She was close to the type I would have automatically started hitting on within ten seconds back in my pathetic single days. These days, I still looked, *briefly*, without giving much more than a second thought. Sure, she was cute. But *my* girl eclipsed them all. It wasn't even close.

I suppose if I'd spoken that opinion aloud, I would have gotten razzed for sounding hokey. Since I still had my persona to maintain, I kept those kinds of thoughts inside my head.

But I definitely would avail myself of this concierge's services—not *those* services. But she could definitely help me on my quest to return from this trip with a fiancée instead of a girlfriend.

April had been hinting for a while now what she thought the direction of our relationship should be. And terrified as I was of that particular step, I wanted nothing more than to make her happy. Yep, here I was, Jordan Guy Fawkes, ready, willing, and able to put a ring on it. And I'd do my level best to ignore the internal screaming of the reformed rakehell.

Because it was time to make this woman mine for good.

And I was determined to do it in a way that would be outstanding, unique and unforgettable. A memory that she would savor forever. I wanted her to waggle her fingers under the light, to show off her massive rock. I wanted to hear her recount with a dreamy, almost breathless voice how her husband-to-be had dropped to one knee and slipped it on her finger while violins played our song and birds tweeted her name.

Damn, even the thought made my heart palpitate and sweat form on my brow, in twenty-five degree weather here on the side of the mountain.

Snow bunny concierge and her male assistant led our way into the massive place—a seven-bedroom mansion with industrial kitchen, self-service wet bar, billiard room, gaming room, library, indoor sauna, and jacuzzi. Every bedroom had its own fireplace, TV with fully equipped sound system, balcony, walk-in closets and ensuite bathroom. Adam and Mia had set us up in style, and I was duly impressed.

This vacation would be the perfect moment to pop the question—here, adjacent to the very city where our romance had begun... more or less.

Our room had a lovely view overlooking the valley and the village. *Breathtaking. Gorgeous. Stunning.* The view? No, my girlfriend's tight little ass in spandex as she bent over to go through the drawers. Damn, I had to get her into bed, stat, because this little outfit of hers was making me hornier than an Adderall-addicted pubescent teen with a stolen copy of vintage *Hustler* and a bottle of pre-warmed lotion.

"Look at this! They unpacked for us already. So cool. Everything is so nicely organized, too. So what should we do first? Ski? Hot tub? Sauna? This place has it all."

I gave her a lusty grin. "Hot sex?"

"We do that all the time."

"So? We have never done it *here*. In this room, with that view. Like... imagine being pressed up against that window while we are getting freaky."

"That window would be negative one hundred degrees Kelvin, and my nips would never take being freeze-dried. So no."

I didn't bother correcting her that there was no such thing as negative one hundred degrees Kelvin. I knew that fact, but I'd never state it aloud. That was something that nerds like Adam or even Lucas would do. Not me. No, I'd just play up my obsession with my girl's perfect ass because... it was, indeed, perfect. As were her boobs, her tiny waist. Those legs...

You get the picture.

But it begged the question... Where the hell was I going to stash this rock where she wouldn't find it? I scanned the room, searching for any nook or cranny that wouldn't be obvious. It was pristine in here, all clean lines, modern furniture and décor. Almost as minimalist as the shared areas were cozy.

I'd definitely have to wait until she left the room to make the move, anyway. But right now, she was busy gawking at the superb view out our window. Maybe I could just whip it out and get on my knee now and get the whole thing over with? What a relief that would be—like pulling out a loose tooth or ripping off a band-aid. I guess those weren't the best visuals to equate asking the woman of my dreams to become my... um... *wife*.

Fuck, I couldn't even get it out seamlessly in my thoughts. It might require some practice before actually vocalizing it. Was I really so averse to the idea of marriage, or was this part of the persona that I'd adopted so long ago? I'd been engaged once before—when I was still a child and didn't know any better. It hadn't gone well, to the tune of finding my ex-fiancée naked underneath some biker bad boy piece of shit in her dorm room. *In flagrante delicto*, or whatever that Latin term was for "right in the middle of bumping uglies like wild beasts in rut." *Jesus*.

I'd learned, then and there, never ever to surprise a person ever again. Yet here I was, planning to do just that. With a ring she'd never laid eyes on.

A few weeks ago I'd dragged Adam on a little excursion with me after a meeting in LA. He had not been thrilled about being dragged away from work to be sent on a fool's errand. And that's exactly what I was, too. *A fucking fool.*

But hey, it had been over a year since I'd realized that April was the girl for me, so it was time to get this shit done. Jump over that cliff yelling *Banzai!* while also screaming like a scared little girl all the way down.

Adam had given me that look before I'd dragged him into the Tiffany's in Beverly Hills. "I dunno, man. Why don't you ask her mom? That's what I did. Kim knew Emilia's taste way better than I did. What better person to ask?"

I'd rubbed at my chin and sent him a quick glance out of the corner of my eye. "No can do. Her mom is... um... a psycho and they don't speak." That's about all I'd share of *that.* I mean, I could have called her a "cougar from Hell" but I'd restrained myself.

Fortunately, in the almost two years that we'd been together, Mommie Dearest had not attempted to break the fool-proof perimeter that we'd set up to keep her out—blocked phone number, blocked social media, all mutual acquaintances and relatives notified. She might have found a way if she'd wanted to, but she hadn't tried.

"Okay," Adam gestured almost impatiently. "What about *your* mother, then? Mothers are way better at this shit than I'd be."

"My mother lives two hundred miles away and besides... I kind of want to present to this to my parents as a done deal. You know..."

He frowned. "I thought the friction was with your dad, and you're on good terms with your mom?"

I shrugged. "I am. But it's just better this way. I'd prefer they both find out after the fact. That way, Mom can soften the blow on the old man. Not that he really cares, mind you."

"Don't they like April?"

I laughed. "They both absolutely love her, actually. But the old man has been acting like a prick to me for years."

Adam shook his head and laughed. "Whoever thought you'd have to think strategically about how to announce your engagement to your parents?" Yeah, well, he had no parents to speak of—that I was aware of—and an uncle who was married to the mother of his wife, so he really hadn't had to worry about it. I guess there were some advantages to being an orphan, though I'd never say that to Adam, because clearly the disadvantages outweighed the advantages in his life.

I made a dramatic gesture. "I'm just sayin' this isn't as easy as marrying a cousin, like you did."

He rolled his eyes and blew out a breath of disgust. "You want my help or not, asshole? I'm not putting up with the cousin jokes today."

"Okay, fine. Just let me know when you two are ready to pull up and move to the Ozarks to start rearing your inbred brood."

Adam immediately pointed to a ring. "Get her a big rock. Women like big rocks."

"Well, there's all this shit about cut and carats and clarity and whatnot."

"Do you have an idea of how much you want to spend? Get her the biggest rock you can possibly get for the price. Size matters when it comes to diamonds."

"Who are we kidding? Size matters in all cases."

Adam gave me side-eye. "Now you sound like Heath."

"Gay guys had all this shit figured out ages ago, man. We hets are knuckle-draggers compared to them."

Soon as a salesperson got involved, there was all the confusing talk of carats, clarity, cut. I opted for pear-shaped because the greasy used-car salesperson-type (took one to know one, I'd admit) had said that was one of the best shapes to show off size. This thing was going to cover her finger from knuckle to knuckle and shine like a comet every time she moved. She'd feel like a movie star or a kept woman or...

I guess obsessing over the ring was helping me forget that I was actually going to ask her to become my wife. Forever and ever. And ever. *Gulp.*

I was ready for this, right? Ready to be a.... um... a husband?

Well, here went nothing. I just had to figure out the exact, beautiful moment to do it. And until then, I'd guard the ring like a convict trying to smuggle a bag of Oxy into prison.

Huh, why was that the first analogy to pop into my head? *Curious.*

Who could hold on to the ring for me in the meantime? Adam was a definite possibility, but he was still extra cranky about being dragged into the store to buy the damn thing in the first place. In addition, there was the added risk of Mia discovering it and letting slip to April that she'd seen it. *No bueno.*

William? He was, after all, deeply responsible. I could trust him to get the job done, especially if I framed it as a quest to guard the princess's jewels or some such. The problem was that the guy was shit at lying, and if discovered on his person, he'd blurt out everything.

Lucas? Maybe... but again, what cover story could he possibly use if Katya found him holding onto a big fat diamond ring when he was already married?

No, the best bet was to carry it on me and hope she kept her hands off my sexy, irresistible bod before I could stash it somewhere in the room. Which meant *soon.* When the hell was she going to use the bathroom, so I could do this?

Damn. I was already losing it, and I hadn't even planned out how to pop the question yet.

I wasn't made for this shit.

# CHAPTER 4
## *APRIL*

MY BEAST WAS ACTING SO WEIRD, LIKE... CRAZY nervous. He'd been on edge for the past few weeks, as a matter of fact, but I'd been so pre-occupied with my thesis for my MBA that I hadn't yet had the time to dig into it.

I frowned, catching glimpses of him as the concierge showed us around our mansion home for the next week. Usually when I approached him too directly, Jordan got skittish and clammed up. But since we'd have this time together this week, I hoped to get to the bottom of it using my subtle arts of Beast-taming. Hopefully it wasn't anything too serious or permanent...

Maybe something was going on at work that I didn't know about?

Jordan had confided in me not long ago. He suspected Adam might be preparing to move on from being CEO of Draco. I couldn't even imagine it, since this company was Adam's baby. But he did have a lot of other interests—including his work with that XVenture company that was sending their own astronauts into space. Adam had been working so hard on those projects that a lot of the CEO duties for Draco were now falling on Jordan's desk.

It was no mystery to me what Jordan wanted, provided it was true that Adam would soon be moving on. Jordan wanted that CEO job, and I'd be more than thrilled to see him get it.

Maybe that was the reason he was so jumpy? It was possible Adam had confided in him and he hadn't had a chance to fill me in, or he was waiting for a time to break it to me. I couldn't imagine Jordan keeping that secret from me for very long. I'd weasel it out of him somehow.

Brushing my hands together as if dusting them off some hard work, I said, "Well, since I don't have to unpack and we aren't doing anything organized until lunch, I think I'll wander out and explore the place, maybe see how the girls are doing. Someone's gotta make sure they didn't get better rooms than we did."

Jordan laughed that fake laugh he only used when trying to blow off a business contact or annoying person. Hmm. What was that? I frowned and left the bedroom.

Mia was out in the main lounge, the large couches almost swallowing up her form. This mansion was breathtaking, with cathedral ceilings reaching up two stories to provide for massive walls of glass overlooking the slopes and the snow-covered valley below. The mountains dominated the horizon, softened by clumps of forest bordering the ski track. I was a decent skier and Jordan adored snowboarding. He was a natural on the snowboard, actually, having grown up on a surfboard. We were both excited to get up on the mountain tomorrow.

"This place is amazing," I breathed as I plopped down opposite Mia. She looked up from her tablet, almost bleary eyed and oblivious to the opulence around her. In fact, she seemed barely aware of my presence until I'd spoken to her.

"Huh? Oh yeah. Did you see there's an indoor pool and jacuzzi? And even an infrared sauna on the bottom floor. I've been dying to try one of those."

"Oh my gawd, a sauna? That sounds like heaven. Saunas are great for the skin." I patted my cheeks. "I could use a little revitalizing."

Mia's brow crinkled. "You're stunning and have the most amazing glowing skin I've ever seen. What are you even talking about right now?"

I shrugged, warmed by the compliment. You had to love Mia. She had no affectation whatsoever, despite her own gorgeous looks. She and Adam turned heads when they were together, effortlessly emanating power-couple vibes in waves. I'd spied people gawking at them like they were celebrities.

"You know," I said as I adjusted myself on the couch, stretching my legs out along it and swiveling sideways. "I'm probably the only person on this entire trip who's not going to berate you for bringing your schoolwork with you, since I brought mine, too."

Mia gave me a guilty look, and then scanned the huge room. "I feel like a hypocrite. Please don't rat me out. I made Adam lock up his phone."

"I'd never tattle. Your secret's safe with me."

The doorbell rang then.

I arched a brow. "You mean this place doesn't come with a butler to answer the door for us?" With a smile, Mia sighed and set her tablet down, but I popped up faster and motioned for her to stay put.

"I'll get it. Probably the concierge."

But it wasn't.

The dude on the other side of the door projected anything *but* at-your-service vibes. My eyes slid up from the Christian Dior après-ski boots to the M. Miller base layers and bespoke Montcler coat, all wrapped around one very impressive male form. The tall, dark, and delightfully wealthy man standing on the front porch was drop-dead gorgeous to boot. Dark, curling hair, *check.* Mysterious gray eyes, *check and wow.*

Okay, so I was spoken for. *Happily* so. But this girl wasn't dead, either, and you'd *have* to be dead not to notice this guy. I blinked. "Uh, um. May I help you?" I squeaked.

His handsome face split into a lazy grin. *Whoa.* He exuded confidence, wealth and some sort of *je ne sais quoi.* Elegance? I half expected a European accent to come out of that sexy mouth of his.

But alas, when he spoke, he sounded perfectly, normally, American. "I was just dropping in to say hello to my friend Adam Drake. Is he in by any chance?"

"Uhhh." I turned from the doorway to glance toward the couch, but Mia was no longer there. Nope, she'd zipped up beside me, quick as a flash, her cheeks flushed pink.

"He had to step out for a few minutes," Mia said. "He doesn't have his phone with him, or I'd text, but can I help you? Please, come in. I'm Mrs. Drake."

His dark brows raised, and he leaned forward to shake her hand. "So good to meet you, finally. My name's Dominic. Adam and I once worked together and when I heard he was here, I had to drop by and grab a chance to catch up. I'd love to invite you for dinner one of the nights you're in town. Speak to him and let me know what fits best with your schedule." Then he reached into his très expensive jacket and pulled out a card to hand to her.

I frowned. This guy looked familiar, and not just in a "man of a girl's dreams" sort of way. Damn. There was a sure bet I was Googling this dude the second I got his full name off Mia's card.

Mia seemed perplexed as he turned away without another word. A veritable mystery man. She glanced down at the card, then again at his receding back. Once the door was shut, I begged her to see the card.

It had no business logo on it. Plain but thick, cream-colored linen paper with a name, email and phone number.

"Dominic Fischer…." Mia read, then shook her head. "How come I've never heard Adam talk about him?"

"Adam probably knows tons of billionaires."

Her brow arched. "You think he's—"

"From the looks of how he was decked out? Yes. Or close." My fingers were already flying over my phone screen, typing the name into Google. Dom Fischer… even the name was giving me Don Draper vibes.

Damn, how would he look in an Armani suit?

Mia stuffed the card in her pocket. "I better stash that tablet before Adam gets back. But I can always distract him with this card and his long-lost mystery friend."

"And you can pump him for info, too. I'm intrigued."

She grinned. "I'll get the tea and spill it all for you, how's that?"

"Damn, aren't we a couple of gossips?"

Mia laughed. "Yeah, real housewives of Orange County, huh?"

"That would be funnier if I was actually a *wife* or if either of us hung out at our houses much." As I finished speaking, I caught a sudden movement in the kitchen and tilted my head, thinking it might be Adam come in through the side door. He could get us the juicy deets…

But no, it was Jordan standing in front of the fridge, his delicious butt begging to be squeezed in those tight jeans. I sighed. Yeah, I could look at another guy and appreciate hotness, but nothing compared to the hotness I already had.

Jordan turned and stared at me, probably alarmed when I'd said I wasn't a wife. How fun. I'd punked him without even realizing I was doing it. I'd gotten so good at teasing him about the whole marriage thing that I was now doing it subconsciously.

"You finding something good to eat in there?" I called after he'd stood motionless in front of the open fridge for way too long.

"Uh, yeah. Anna stocked this up good for us. She's amazing, that Anna."

Huh. Amazing? That saucy blonde concierge had openly drooled all over my Beast since the minute she'd met us until the moment she'd left for the morning. As she'd shown us around the mansion, I'd found it necessary to hang off Jordan's arm and be all lovey and demonstrative just so she'd get the point.

She made her own point of checking out my left hand—and not even hiding the fact she was doing it, either. Then she was all smiles and giggles whenever he talked.

For real, my Beast was a very tempting hunk of meat, and I couldn't always be around to fight off the she-vultures. But I was here, now, and Anna would soon get the clue that not only was I not going anywhere, but I didn't take kindly to others messing with what was mine. I was the lioness on the savannah defending her juicy kill from opportunistic hyenas.

I studied him through narrowed eyes as he grabbed an apple out of the fridge, washed it and then sauntered off with it in his hand.

Mia had grabbed her tablet and disappeared into her room, and here I was, alone.

I stuffed my phone in my pocket, vowing to find out more about the mystery man later but deciding to concentrate on the current mystery of what was eating Jordan.

Maybe he needed a little of my sugar to take the edge off?

It had the bonus of keeping him sexually satisfied to the point of exhaustion so that he'd be too fatigued to even look at Anna.

Yes, I think a mind-blowing BJ, as soon as possible, would be just what the doctor ordered. Anna was cute, but I was cuter and *I* got to share his bed every night. So take that, Snow Bunny Sue.

I was not weak of heart when some hyena zeroed in on my hunk of meat. I rose to the occasion, claws out and ready to go for the jugular. Over my dead lioness body. I had mine. She'd have to go hunting in some other savannah to find hers.

And I'd waste no time getting that point unmistakably across to her.

# Chapter 5
## Jenna

ELL, IT HAD TAKEN LESS THAN A FULL DAY FOR ME to realize that the mountains really agreed with me.

Sitting by the fire amidst the hustle and bustle of late morning just after breakfast, I thought I could spend a multitude of days here with my closest friends, my sweetie sitting beside me quietly reading a magazine he'd found on the coffee table.

*Knit two rows, purl two rows.* I was in the middle of purling when I slipped up and knit one on the wrong row. With a heavy sigh, I undid the stitch and redid it correctly.

I was a newbie knitter, so it was slow going. And though I was using homespun wool I'd bartered off one of my friends in our barony of the Medieval Reenactment Alliance, I had no intention of going near period-appropriate knitting needles. Instead, I'd picked up modern metal needles from the local craft store. Knit... no purl. I was purling this row again. The alternating knitting and purling two rows was producing a nice ribbed texture in the wool.

I was so close to being done, but I'd been beyond silly to think I'd have this scarf done for William in time for Christmas. Overly ambitious. I'd started at Thanksgiving, thinking a month would be plenty of time... *haha, no.*

Between my first year of teaching at a real job, spending time with William, and our participation in the Medieval Reenactment society, we were actually very busy. I squeezed in knitting a few rows here and there while I was waiting at appointments or watching TV—which, since Wil wasn't the biggest fan of watching, wasn't very often. Sometimes I'd get a few rows done in bed before falling asleep.

It hadn't been enough time. So on Christmas Eve, I'd had to give up and wrap it unfinished, and put it under the tree—needles, yarn and all. When he'd opened it the next day, he'd been more than a little confused. Maybe he'd thought I'd expected him to finish it. He'd probably pick it up faster than I had... He had mad skills with his hands. In *every* way....

I could feel him watching me. It was a secret talent of mine—to know when I was being watched. William had been looking over the edge of that magazine, staring at my work for minutes now. I braced myself.

"Is the magazine boring?" I asked.

"It's not what I usually read," he replied in his characteristic monotone. "But there are some interesting articles."

"Then why are you watching me knit instead of reading them?"

He shrugged. "The articles aren't as interesting as you are. Also, you dropped a stitch, three stitches back."

I sighed and checked. Of course he was right. I pulled the three complete stitches off my right needle, undid them and slipped them back onto my left needle. "I'll get better at it."

"The fiber arts are difficult to master. In the middle ages, an apprentice studied for three years before becoming a journeyman. It'll take time for you to get good."

I clenched my jaw. Of course, he didn't mean for his critique to sting. Nevertheless, for some reason, it did. This had been a difficult fall. My first one teaching a pack of unruly freshmen in high school. Physical science. They didn't care about the subject at all, and most of them zoned out in class—or worse, they acted out. I'd had to go to great lengths to learn how to entertain them. They were annoying, but teaching was fun.

In spite of that, I came home almost every day exhausted and loaded down with papers to grade and notebooks to plan future lessons. Experiments to design, experiment supplies to order and organize, extra-curricular activities to supervise.... The work was never-ending.

I'd even brought work with me on this trip, on the odd chance that I might have a moment to get something done. But at the moment, this scarf was my sole focus. It was already several days late. Besides, he could use this scarf to keep him warm while we were up here. As Southern Californians, we didn't have many occasions to wear warm clothes—and thus didn't have many thick coats and gloves for those occasions. He definitely needed this..

Only a few dozen more rows... did it really have to be that long anyway, to wrap around his neck? I glanced up at him. My boyfriend was tall, handsome, and powerfully built. His work as our clan's blacksmith, along with his continuing practice of sword fighting while wearing a full suit of armor, had helped him develop a very fit body. He was delicious. But his neck was rather muscular. A few dozen more rows it was, then. A scarf that was too short would be useless.

"I'm practicing. That's what this is all about. Plus, losing a few stitches here or there makes it unique looking."

"It will also cause it to unravel," he helpfully observed.

I could feel my shoulders slump.

He wandered off not too long after that, and I continued to toast my toes by the fire and work my rows. Lucas sank down next to me about an hour later with a resort brochure in his hand.

"Are you looking forward to hitting the slopes?"

He shrugged. "I'm on my wife's turf, now. I just don't want to embarrass her out there."

I laughed. "Well, maybe she'd take kindly to that. She could show you the ropes—if she or you don't break your necks."

His mouth twisted. "Got any ideas on safer ways to say *I love you?*"

My eyes zeroed in on my work as I responded. "Have you tried just telling her those three magical words?"

He smiled. "I actually make a point of those being the last three words I say to her every night before we go to sleep."

My needles faltered. *Awwwww.* Cue my heart melting. That was so incredibly sweet.

Who'd have thought that Lucas, until recently so well-known for his cantankerous grumpiness, could be so transformed by finding the love of his heart? It was enough to make me jealous about new love.

I mean, I had love. I loved my sweetie dearly. And there was no man kinder, sexier, or more chivalrous than William. But when was the last time he'd actually said the words *I love you* to me? Definitely not every night before bed. Not even every week.

I frowned, now seriously considering that question. When *had* the last time been, anyway?

I glanced over at him across the room. He was sitting in the window seat overlooking a gorgeous mountain vista behind him, the sun gleaming on the freshly fallen snow. His dark head was craned over his sketchbook, pencil moving a mile a minute, brow furrowed in concentration. Damn, he was hot.

I bit my lip. Did he still love me? He never said it. Why didn't he ever say it?

Should I be worried?

I pondered that question and kept on knitting.

# CHAPTER 6
# WILLIAM

I SQUINT, ATTEMPTING TO DECIPHER JENNA'S HASTY writing on the wide index card. I normally dislike reading cursive, but her cursive is typically even and lovely. *This* writing is not. She copied it in a hurry, almost as a last-minute idea.

Fortunately, the concierge found the ingredients she requested. And here we are in the kitchen assembling ingredients for the *medenjaci* traditional winter cakes made in Bosnia and Croatia around this time of year. Honey and gingerbread. Of course, honey. When I spent a month with Jenna in her home country almost two years ago, I noticed that most of their treats were sweetened with honey. It's a different taste. Earthy, sweet but full-bodied, unlike cakes sweetened with sugar. I'm looking forward to tasting these, even though Jenna has never made them before.

My job, she has said, is to convert the metric measurements into the American system. However, since we're in Canada, we've discovered that the available baking implements are also in metric. No conversion necessary. How lucky, she says. I remark that I don't believe luck had anything to do with it.

She gives me one of those looks. I've learned what they mean. She's not quite exasperated. Maybe a little frustrated. She's putting a lot of pressure on herself to get these cookies right. Since she's the only Bosnian here, only she will know if she got them wrong.

"I've never baked these by myself before. I've always had Mama to help."

"I don't doubt they will taste delicious. And since you don't need me to convert ingredients, I can go—"

"No!" she says, reaching for my hand and squeezing it. "I need you here."

"For what purpose? I'm not experienced with baking. I have nothing to contribute to this process."

"For moral support, Wil. Company. Someone to talk to while I'm baking."

I raise my brows. "Will that help them taste better?"

She sighs and there's a strange smile on her face. I'm not sure if it's ironic or if she truly is happy. "It will make me happy if you stay."

I frown, ready to formulate my rebuttal but... I have none, to be honest. How can I argue with what makes her happy and what doesn't? After all, she's the best judge of that. And I've been getting better at it, studying her a lot, her reactions to things I do for her. I repeat the ones that get the most obvious reaction. Cleaning the kitchen and doing the dishes is a big one. So perhaps that's why she needs me here. I'll clean up after her as she bakes.

"You should have just taken a picture of the recipe in the book so I could read the ingredients to you."

She raises her brows at me. "You can't read my writing? It is a little sloppy because I was writing fast. I had the idea to make the cookies for everyone at the very last minute. But Mama wrote the recipe in Bosnian in the email, and it wasn't printing. I had to copy and translate it at the same time. All while you were howling at me that we were going to be late for our pickup."

"I wasn't howling. I was—"

She holds up her hand. "It was a joke. But you were being a time tyrant."

A joke. I'm getting better at detecting them, especially from her. "Fine. You may address me as Emperor Expeditious."

"How about punctual pundit?" Her grin widens, and she stirs the wet ingredients more vigorously.

"Punctuality pundit is actually much more accurate than time tyrant."

She smiles again and nods while continuing to stir the batter, rechecking the recipe and occasionally tasting. She's so beautiful. I never get tired of looking at her. And watching her bake is by no means boring. But... I'm itching to get back to my project. I fold my arms and tuck my hands under them to keep them still. I'll force myself not to think about it. There's still plenty of time to get it done.

"I need a few more ingredients. Nutmeg, ginger, and salt. Wanna grab those for me?"

"I can measure out the salt. How many milliliters?"

"Uh..." she squints at the card and her own writing. I refrain from commenting because I know it will get me another look. "She said a pinch of salt and a couple grates of nutmeg."

"What? That's not milliliters."

She shrugs. "Mama makes this recipe a lot. She just... you know... feels it."

I blink at her, horrified. "*Feels* it? A recipe is a chemical formula. How do you *feel* it?"

"Mama has done all the baking, every holiday since before I was born. She taught Maja and I, but of course, I was very little. At least she has Maja now to help her. But I remember the flavors so vividly, and I've missed these things.... When I told Kat I was going to make these, she volunteered to make some Canadian dessert called a Nanaimo bar. So I want these to turn out good."

I read over the card again while she offers me a taste of the batter. I shake my head no because I'd rather taste the finished product.

"I don't understand this recipe. Are you sure you're reading it right?"

She nods and continues on as if she hasn't actually heard me. "I think next we'll do the walnut cakes. Mama also emailed that one to me, but it's still in Bosnian. I'll have to look up some words because I don't remember them."

I frown. "Is that recipe as imprecise as this one? How can your mother possibly repeat her creations, much less pass them on to her daughters, if she can't come up with specific measurements for her food?"

Jenna rolls her eyes and sighs heavily. I know that look too. Exasperation. "It's just guidelines."

"You mean like the Pirate Code is just guidelines? Don't get me started on that movie because—"

"William!" she says, folding her arms across her chest and standing stiffly. She never calls me by my full name. It's either Wil or sweetie. I like both of those much better coming from her. I don't care for her exasperation, though.

"You've been a great help, but you can go now. I just have to start popping these in the oven. I think I'm good," she says with a long sigh.

I straighten. "Leave the dishes for me to clean."

And then I happily turn to leave the kitchen while she scoops dough onto a cookie sheet. Good. I need to get back to that project. The more time I can spend on it, the better it will turn out. I have to grab every minute I can to work on it. We're due to leave for dinner in Whistler Village in just over an hour. Fortunately, it's at a casual diner and I won't have to take time to get dressed up for it.

Before leaving, I turn back. "I'm here to help taste them when they are done."

"Of course you are," she replies as I leave.

# CHAPTER 7
## *KATYA*

I T WAS WINTER IN MY BEAUTIFUL FORMER HOME OF BRITISH Columbia, and I had the rare opportunity to enjoy Whistler like a one-percenter. All because my BFF and her hubby were actual, generous one-percenters who liked to share with their friends. I was nothing but over-the-top impressed by our beautiful mansion. And the food! The caterer had already made us several meals to die for.

So what the hell were we doing in this little après-ski diner for dinner tonight?

Apparently, it was so everyone could try poutine and mock me about it. What else was new?

"If I lived in Canada, I'd have a pet moose just so I could name him Bullwinkle," Jordan snorted. Ha ha. A moose joke. Never heard anything like *that* before. Eye roll.

The waiter arrived with several orders of poutine. Plates overflowing with heaps of fries piled high on a plate covered with white chunks of cheese curd and a rich, flavorful gravy. It wasn't even something that western Canadians had regularly enjoyed until very recently. Poutine was a product of Quebec, and *this* western Canadian was not a fan.

"Here we go! I've been dying to try this."

Mia stared at the plate as if trying to figure out what the hell it was. "*That's* poutine?"

"It's not a food." Jordan's snide voice cut in. "It's the culinary equivalent of having unprotected sex with a prostitute in a truck stop."

I raised my brows. "Speaking from experience, Jordan?"

Adam had already helped himself to several bites of the gooey fries. "Damn, this stuff tastes way better than it looks."

"That's good, because it looks like someone had intestinal problems all over that plate," Heath cut in.

"Gross!" whined April.

"What's not to like?" Adam gestured to the plate. "French fries? Goood. Cheese? Gooooood! Gravy? Gooooood. Put it all together and you have poutine." He turned to his wife. "C'mon, girl. Time to try the food of your best friend's people, eh?"

Mia pointed straight at me. "*She* doesn't even like it. Why would I like it? My lipoprotein panel would be off the charts if I ate that." Mia shook her head vehemently. "I'm definitely going to run it on you if you keep eating it."

"Sounds kinky." Heath smirked and waggled his brows. "Oh, what the hell… Might as well get my Letterkenny on." He leaned forward and stuffed a clump of fries into his mouth. *Traitor.*

Adam wasn't done taunting Mia, waving a lone, gravy-soaked fry in front of her face. "Sometimes you need to walk on the wild side."

She winked at him. "I save my wild side for the bedroom, and I haven't heard any complaints from you."

"Get a room," Jordan said.

I sipped my delicious Canadian beer—gawd how I'd missed it!—and shook my head at the fools I called friends. Mercifully, my husband was staying silent and not joining in on the taunts.

Strange how things worked out. Here I was, in Canada, with all of my closest friends. And not only were we all in my country of origin, but we were less than two hundred kilometres from where I'd grown up. Was this week going to be full of my friends taking potshots at Canada? Because I wanted out, now. Or I'd have to shut them up by firing back. And Jordan would be my number one target.

"Hey Kat," snorted Jordan. "Did you hear about that terrible case of Canadian graffiti? Someone spray-painted 'Sorry about your wall.'"

"Hey Jordan," I leaned forward in my chair, preparing to volley back. "Did you hear that when god created Canada, he decided to create the most perfect, beautiful country with breathtaking natural scenery, bountiful resources, and really nice people. When one of his angels told him it wasn't fair to give Canada all of that, God said 'Wait 'til I create their obnoxious, loud, and entitled neighbors. That'll make up for it.'"

"Ooooh burn." Adam chuckled.

"Feisty Canadian redhead is feisty." Jordan grabbed a gravy-slathered fry and popped it in his mouth. "I'm not trying to hurt your feelings, Kat."

"No worries. We're in Canada. I can always visit the doctor to get checked for hurt feelings—at no charge." Jenna held up a hand, and I slapped a high five on it while the rest of the table chuckled.

April looked up from the information guide she'd been studying on her phone. "So, if my dear, beloved boyfriend will stop his teasing for five minutes, maybe Kat can tell us what the best slopes are to ski around here? I imagine, being a Vancouverite, you've skied here often?"

I hadn't skied very often growing up. Skiing required money, and that wasn't in huge supply at our house. Lift tickets cost your eye teeth, to say nothing of the equipment. I'd owned a secondhand set of skis and boots at one time, but they'd been lost or sold off when I hadn't used them in over two years. Most of the time, when I'd come up to Whistler with friends, it had been to hang around the village, go to bars or dancing, and meet guys.

But after getting needled by Jordan, I wasn't about to admit to the whole table that I was, at best, a mediocre skier.

I coughed. "Oh yeah, I used to come up all the time, but it's been a long time, so I'm sure everything has changed. What does the guide recommend?"

She rattled off her answer—a few of the names were ones my skiing friends had mentioned in the past. I nodded along.

Finally, our meal arrived. I'd ordered Breakfast for Dinner, complete with a stack of pancakes because I'd been dying to get my hands on some honest-to-god *real* maple syrup, and here was my chance to bathe my dinner in it.

"Nothing's complete without maple syrup," I sighed happily.

"True story. I even caught her putting it in her coffee once. I'll know we're in real trouble when she starts brushing her teeth with it," Lucas drawled. The first words out of his mouth all night and they were to join in on the teasing. Everyone laughed, and Jordan mumbled something about Canucks. I glared at my husband through narrowed eyes for restarting the pile-on. I thought he was supposed to be on my side? At least him, I could punch.

So I did.

He gave me a dirty look and rubbed his arm, but kept his mouth shut. Mission accomplished. Next, I'd have to threaten to withhold my wifely favors, but he'd know in a heartbeat that I was bluffing. I wouldn't be able to hold out any longer than he could. That threat never went anywhere. Probably a good thing. Withholding the favors meant no fun for me, either.

"Lucas, I can imagine you're quite the skier, what with your upbringing," April said.

Lucas flashed me a look of dismay, still annoyed that I'd spilled all the info about his upper crust upbringing complete with aristocratic European title. But who could blame me? I'd secretly married the guy, and *then* I'd found out I was a baroness!

*Of course* I was going to brag about that shit to my friends!

I grinned at him. "Didn't you ski in Austria with the Dutch Royal Family?"

"One time. Once." He blew out a breath and rolled his eyes, clearly regretting having let that tidbit about his past drop when he'd had a bit too much Scotch.

April was staring from one of us to the other, her eyes widening. It was almost as if she couldn't believe her ears, and to be honest, if I were in her position, I'd probably feel the same way.

Jordan seemed to notice her reaction, eyes flicking from first her to Lucas and then me, and back, and then that devilish grin teased his mouth. I recognized that grin. Having worked with him as long as I had, I knew what it meant. He was up to something.

"It seems we've got one spouse from Canada, practically raised in the shadow of one of the best ski resorts in North

America. The other one cut his teeth all over the Alps and Pyrenees. It would be interesting to see how a friendly competition between you two would end up."

Lucas's eyes narrowed suspiciously at his friend. Me, on the other hand, I kept my gaze on my plate, suddenly fascinated with my pancakes.

"I mean, aren't you two even a little bit curious? You know, for the sake of your progeny. Who knows, you might even end up raising an Olympian one day."

I barked out a laugh at the ridiculous thought. Lucas's brown eyes flicked to me and then back at Jordan. "We're not like that. We don't compete all the time."

I almost choked on my food. We were completely and totally competitive as gamers. *Everybody* knew this about us.

"What about a little friendly competition between spouses?" Jordan still had that gleam in his eye, the fucker. What on earth was he trying to accomplish? Only the shit-stirrer, himself, knew that.

I'd never seen Lucas ski, but I could only imagine that, having been raised in his noble richy-rich family that visited high-end ski resorts across the world, he would easily show up my mediocre skills.

I rolled my eyes. "Oh, yeah. All Canadians are practically born on skis. They start screening for Olympic hopefuls in elementary school. I was earmarked, but my parents didn't want to spend the money. Anyway, I got bored with it when I got my driver's license and a boyfriend." I took a sip of water with a snarky smile and glanced up to see who was gullible to have bought it.

Answer? By the looks on their shocked faces, all of them. Were Yankees all this gullible?

Lucas's brows raised almost to his hairline. My mind raced for a quick segue to change the subject. "So, anyway, the poutine–"

"Wait, you can't just drop something like that." Jordan leaned forward, his hand gesturing.

"Yes, I can. I just did." Might as well take it to the next level while they were still lapping it up, right? I wondered how much mileage I could get out of this. "It's painful to discuss, really, that my future was so altered by my family's poverty." I punctuated this with a wistful sigh, then added a glance to the side as if to emphasize my point of regret. I could all but keep myself from busting up laughing.

I'd clue them in later… maybe way later after they'd shut up with their dumb jokes.

"So is it on, then?" Jordan pushed.

I tossed a casual shrug with one shoulder and affected my most obvious bored face. The more uninterested and nonchalant I acted with this, hopefully the sooner all this talk of skiing competitions and racing would go away.

What was this anyway, *Steep and Deep?* The K12 race in *Better Off Dead?* Or even *Hot Tub Time Machine?*

"Oh, my husband is well aware of the fact that I can ski better than him."

"I am?"

I darted Lucas a meaningful look. If he'd just play along with me, this BS would go away, and we could shut Jordan up once and for all—a nearly impossible feat most times.

"Jordan's not wrong." Adam leaned in. "You could prove this pretty easily and quickly." *Oh shit.* When Adam spoke, Lucas listened. And that meant he might actually get egged into this stupid thing.

"We *could*." I shrugged and sniffed, digging deep into the indifference I didn't actually feel. "I just don't want to humiliate my *sugar buns*." I emphasized the pet name and put my hand on his shoulder, squeezing tightly. When he met my gaze, I gave him another *look*. Clearly, we hadn't been married long enough to for him to have the foggiest idea what my looks meant, dammit. I suddenly wished I was a telepath who could mentally transmit my commands to my chosen life partner.

Lucas stared, brow wrinkling in puzzlement. As if I could see it, the point went whizzing over his head like lasers beams shot from the blasters of Storm Troopers. *Ah, married life.*

"So, it's settled then," Jordan said with a grin. "We're going to have a spousal ski-off. Which run do you want to do, The Coffin or Couloir Extreme?"

"Oh," I laughed. "I used to do those runs when I was in middle school. They were fun." I waved my hand again breezily while silently wishing Jordan would break his leg on his first ski run tomorrow. Or better yet, his jaw, so he couldn't talk anymore.

Jordan looked up from his map of the mountain runs, eyebrow arching. "We can pick one at random, then, and you can do it? Maybe we should handicap you to give your poor husband a chance. What about a blindfold?"

"I can handle this just fine." Lucas darted me a challenging look. "I think I'm perfectly able to kick her ass fair and square."

"Ooooooh!" The rest of the table leaned in, some shaking their hands at the wrists. What the hell had I just gotten myself into? *Crappity crap.* These idjits had hung on my every word, my every bluff like it was gospel. I'd been so annoyed by all the

Canada shit-talking that I'd let my own big mouth write checks I was certain my body—and skiing ability—couldn't cash.

Now, these so-called friends of ours were slobbering at the chance to rubberneck at the weird ski-off pitting husband against wife. I bit my lip.

Oh, hell. Was I going to have to risk breaking a limb in the name of defeating my husband? With video games, I pulled it off regularly with no threat to my person at all, except for maybe a sprained finger or a little carpal tunnel syndrome.

I swallowed and then just threw another one of those stupid *I'm over it already* shrugs. "I have no problem showing my husband his place."

"Ooooooh!" The table broke out again. Even beyond the cheesy and tired Canadian jokes, this was reminding me more and more of middle school.

Mia shook her head. "You two are worse than Adam and me. I never thought I'd see the day."

"Wait, what's that what the heck is that supposed to mean?" Adam asked.

Mia laughed and patted her husband on the shoulder. "Nothing, dear."

"So it's on, then? I'll be handling the betting pool and doling out odds. Just call me the ski bookie. What day should we do it?" Jordan nudged April, whose eyes slid down the itinerary.

*Oh, hell.*

"Well, there's this block of free time after lunch on the day before New Year's Eve. We have nothing scheduled from one till three. Why not then?"

*Gulp.* "Ah, I—"

"It is *on!*" My husband interrupted me to exclaim, a smug smile playing about his mouth.

"That's what I like to see." Jordan flashed Lucas a thumbs up.

I guess this meant I needed to get practicing or admit my lie now.

Sigh. So practicing it was.

Even if I had to fake breaking my arm at the last minute, I'd see this bluff through to its bitter, bloody—hopefully not literally—end.

# CHAPTER 8
## *LUCAS*

WHAT ABOUT THIS TRIP WAS SUPPOSED TO BE restful and retreat-ish again?

Here I thought I'd be up in the snow, admiring beautiful vistas, sipping hot chocolate and making love with my beautiful wife whenever I wanted.

Instead, I'd been roped into some farcical competition with her, while also dealing with bullshit from work during a week when work had been shut down for the holidays. In addition, my two bosses were also here.

Who'd have thought that becoming the brand-new head of a brand-new company division would more resemble being a therapist and hand-holder of children than a boss myself?

I'd handpicked my own team from within the company and outside of it. Brought in loads of talent for the new virtual reality division of Draco Multimedia Entertainment. But only a few months in, I was dealing with drama. Two of my key creatives were trying to railroad each other.

This meant phone calls, videoconferences, long, wordy, and very detailed emails. Time better used to enjoy my vacation.

Until this stupid ski race. How the hell had that even come about, anyway?

When my wife interrupted my business call the next morning, I slammed my laptop shut, determined to keep the messy details from her. I didn't have the right to rain on her parade. She was doing so well at her new job. Management had created the position and tailored it for her special talents. She was flying high in her new position.

So it would be selfish to spoil her happiness with my own depressing workplace concerns.

"It's almost time for that helicopter tour. Can you believe we're going to fly in a helicopter! I've never even been in one before. Have you?"

I shrugged and gave her a sheepish look. My family had owned one for a while.

"Oh yeah, forgot, Baron Lucas van den Hoehnsboek van Lynden. Of course you have, your eminence and worship," she bowed and made a flourish.

"Whatever, peasant," I said with a grin, my standard reply whenever she teased me about it—which was often. It was either call her peasant or remind her that she was now a baroness by their standard, because she was married to me.

She sobered, biting her lip.

I frowned. "What's wrong?"

"So about this whole ski race—"

"Knock, knock!" Mia poked her head inside our open door while rapping on the door frame. "We're headed to the helicopter in five."

Kat and I nodded at her, and once she disappeared, I turned, expecting Kat to continue her sentence about the stupid ski race that I didn't even want to do.

"Let's talk about it later." She grabbed her jacket and threw me mine. "Time to go pop my helicopter ridin' cherry."

"That's not really the cherry I think about popping—constantly."

She laughed at me, blue eyes crinkling at the corners. "Later, horndawg."

I was too preoccupied with work problems to enjoy the tour.

Maybe it was a good thing we had this bullshit ski competition to focus on. And to keep the bosses focused on. They brought it up every time we were all together, in fact.

I gazed across at my gorgeous wife. She was all smiles and excitement, pointing things out to me and talking over a headset like we were on a Dragon Epoch raid. Who knew that my bride was a champion skier? She was full of surprises. But this one? I never would have thought.

"You two are getting along swimmingly for being pitted against each other in the ultimate intra-marital downhill contest." Jordan's voice, booming dramatically in imitation of a sports commentator, broke in over the speaker.

I shot him an annoyed glance. Damned instigator.

I'd skied before, having visited many prestigious resorts with my family as I was growing up. But that didn't make me an automatic expert. I'd much preferred to be on the water sculling in a racing boat under the sun rowing than whooshing down a slope with icy wind in my hair. Skiing bored me.

But apparently now I was supposed to be serving my wife humble pie on the slopes.

Why didn't I just admit to her that I wasn't that good?

I watched her as her face lit up, taking in the view, the sunlight gleaming in her fiery hair that poured over her shoulders. I could just tell her that this was stupid, confer her the winner, and then even the score in bed—a much more interesting sport than downhill skiing.

But there was now the added problem that my bosses were invested. In fact, I'd seen Jordan's pool sheet, and Kat and I were pretty evenly divided where the bets were concerned.

Saving face or no, it wasn't worth my life. I'd only done a black diamond run a few times in my life, and neither of them had ended well. Mostly they'd wrapped up with me rolling down the slope, screaming at the top of my lungs and threatening avalanches for miles around.

"So, this whole black diamond thing… do you think that's the best way to show off our skills? On a run where no one will be able to see what we're doing? It would probably make more sense to go down the intermediate runs. More opportunity for them to watch us…" I asked Kat as we left the helicopter pad and drifted about twenty feet behind the clump of our friends. Everyone was headed for the SUV and the driver waiting patiently to whisk us to our next fun-filled activity.

"What's wrong, Colonel Sanders, *chicken?*" she quipped with a laugh.

It was just enough to get my ire up. "No. Fine. You want a black diamond race? Fine. Enjoy eating my snow."

Once we caught up with the group, however, and stuffed ourselves into the big car, the conversation rolled over and over in my mind.

She was more likely to make *me* eat *her* snow.

Oh well, at least snow would taste better than eating my own words.

No, I wasn't going to humiliate myself out there. I just needed some practice, and I had approximately six days to get good enough to at least appear competent, anyway.

No big deal if she ended up winning—though I prayed the gloating wouldn't last forever—but I could at least give her some kind of run for her money.

There was just enough time in the schedule for me to do some practice runs on my own. I messaged our concierge to this effect, and she arranged some lift tickets for me to pick up.

This could go well, or this could end really, really badly. It was way too soon to tell which way it would go.

I grabbed coffee and sat at the breakfast table, tucking the phone back into my pocket. I could do my first practice run this morning if I hurried and got some food in me. Kat might not even wake up until after I'd returned.

Only Mia was at the table with me, as it was early. Fortunately, she was lacking in curiosity about where I was going, gazing out the window and daydreaming over her mug of hot tea.

I doubt she even heard me when I told her goodbye and headed for the door.

# CHAPTER 9
# *MIA*

WE WEREN'T EVEN THROUGH THE SECOND FULL DAY of our magical winter holiday anniversary, and already plans were going awry. The house was amazing, luxurious and well-appointed with every indoor activity and comfort we could ever need in the next week until New Year's Day. I hadn't expected everyone to participate in every activity, but as the days progressed, people seemed to be opting out of the itinerary more and more. I hoped this wasn't a trend.

April seemed on edge about something to do with Jordan. Kat and Lucas had been pitted against each other in a ski race. Jenna and William were cute and adorable, as always, but not fully on board with the group activities. Heath just snarked about the schedule twenty-four-seven, despite participating in every one, and admitting—*after* the fact—that he'd enjoyed it.

On top of everything else, my own husband was acting weird *af,* and I had no idea what to do about it. First of all, if I didn't know better, I'd say he'd started on amphetamines recently and was riding a perpetual, frenetic high. Maybe it was withdrawal symptoms from confiscating his phone? Poor dude was clearly addicted to his device, as I'd accused him of many times. Regardless, he'd made no attempts to get it back, nor did he even talk about it at all. He'd surrendered it to me without comment, stoically, and you'd have never known that thing was his constant and unwavering companion.

So maybe that wasn't the reason behind the weird behavior. I sipped my tea and looked out the picture window from the dining table laden with the remains of lunch. The caterer had quietly delivered breakfast and cold lunch early this morning. I'd grabbed a flaky tuna croissant sandwich, and some sliced fruit. Everyone had finished their meal and gone their separate ways, and I was alone again.

I'd handed Adam the business card his mysterious friend had dropped off yesterday, and now he was in our room, making a call on the cell phone he'd borrowed from me.

I sat contemplating, making plans.

I'd been hoping Adam and I would be getting frisky by now. I'd planned and prepared for it, as a matter of fact, having ordered a series of sexy lingerie—a different one for each night we'd be here. Each silky, lacy confection would be successively trashier than the one before it, a sexual advent countdown, until the series culminated on our anniversary night with the infamous Agent Provocateur faux chain-mail bikini. The very same one I'd indulged him with on our wedding night. I hadn't worn it since, specifically saving it for our night alone in our own special retreat. Hopefully, it would have the same effect on him as it had then. I was counting on it, because we were coming out of a dry spell here.

So, last night had been the sapphire lace teddy. Very tasteful and almost bridal-night virgin chaste with a hint of flirty sexiness. I'd waited until he was in bed to make my grand entrance, covered in the matching silky robe. I'd stood by my side of the bed, coughed to pull his attention from the pad of paper he'd been making notes on. Then I struck a pose and slipped the robe flirtatiously off my shoulder, batting my eyes.

He'd watched me, fully alert and interested, while the fire crackled in the background and flurries of fresh snow whispered against the window.

His eyes slid over me, appreciative but not salacious. If I was being honest, I'd admit to wanting a bit of salacious. More than a bit. It had been over a week, on a rare day we'd both been at home one afternoon. I was on my way to a lab, and he'd dropped by the house to grab something before an afternoon meeting in LA. We'd taken quick advantage of the impromptu rendezvous.

And quickies were great and all, but it was about damn time for some hot, steamy, dirty, sexy fun that lasted longer than a fifteen-minute nooner. So I was encouraged when, with a smile, he laid aside his pad and pen and tugged the sheets back for me to slide in and join him.

He was wearing a t-shirt and pajama pants, which, *boo*. I hadn't seen him fully naked in far too long, and it was more than warm enough in here with the fire going and the snug blankets that we'd both be clothed only in our birthday suits very soon.

So the blue lace teddy was just the pregame, but it looked like I'd signaled my intention well enough with it when I pressed my body to his, shivering just a little under the cold sheets and appreciating the warmth radiating off his skin. I leaned in and buried my nose in his collar bone, taking a big whiff. He always smelled so amazing. The material of the t-shirt was so soft, the muscle underneath so hard. I had caught myself an incredibly delicious husband, and I was holding on for dear life, that was for sure.

My nightcap was nibbling on his delectable neck, basking in the surge of hot lust when his whiskered cheek brushed against mine. I attached myself to that neck like a ravenous vampire on a blood bender, and I wasn't going to let go until every square inch was covered with hickies. Mama was *thirsty*, and he was my cuppa ice water in the middle of the desert.

Just as I was angling to climb him like a tree, I suddenly felt him go rigid—and not in the good way. Shockingly, he used his arm to nudge some space between us and I pulled back, eyes widening in shock. What the hell...? Yeah, I spoke that with my eyes. Words not needed.

He smiled. "Hey... how about we... up our romance game? What do you think about that?"

My brows came down in a frown. "Um. Well... that's what I thought I was just doing."

"You were attaching your mouth to my neck like a sucker fish."

I blinked. "And you didn't like it? You usually... I mean... it's been a while..."

"But we've got six nights here. Wouldn't it be a cool idea if we... took it slower?"

Okay, so my head might have jerked around in the most obnoxious double take ever. Adam Drake never turned down sex. Like *ever*. He'd have to be half dead. Maybe his mono was coming back?

I pressed my hand to his forehead to check if he had a fever. "Are you feeling okay?"

He laughed. "I'm fine I just... thought it might be nice if maybe we cuddled, spent a little time looking into each other's eyes, holding hands."

I raised a brow. "How 'bout a little bump and grind instead? Or a *lot* of it?"

"Oh sure, we can do that later. But tonight, we should try to maybe just enjoy each other's company? We can cuddle, maybe watch the fire after we're done looking into each other's eyes. We don't even have to talk. Just enjoy being in bed at the same time. We hardly ever go to bed at the same time."

Stunned, I sank down beside him. My eyes went to the fireplace. The flames licked and danced against the dark stones and brick. Hold hands? Listen to each other breathe? Had the word *cuddle* just voluntarily slipped from this man's lips?

Had we already crossed into middle-aged, flamed-out marriage territory? Were the sparks gone so soon that he didn't want to jump on me like a ravenous wolf on a wounded sheep?

The last thing I said to him before we spent the longest thirty minutes of my married life just staring off into space while holding his hand was, "Who are you and what have you done to my husband, imposter?"

To which he'd only responded with a chuckle. "Let's just try it and see what happens." Which implied that something might actually, you know, happen.

*Spoiler alert*—it didn't. We were snoozing before the hour was out, passed out like exhausted puppies after a full day of frolicking. Maybe that was it. He'd just been too tired. Maybe I hadn't been communicative enough that I'd be willing to do all the work, and all he'd have to do was lay back and enjoy his orgasm.

But no....

That afternoon, he had a full list of activities for us. He'd found a 2,000-piece puzzle and proposed that we go to the upstairs loft where we'd have privacy to work on it alone. From there, we'd be able to look out and watch the falling snow.

With a knowing smile, I surmised that "working on a puzzle" was a euphemism for fitting our bodies together like puzzle pieces. Though the upstairs loft might leave us open to exposure. Maybe the excitement of possibly getting caught was getting his motor running.

Turned out, no. He really did want to work on a puzzle.

I fucking hate puzzles. And he was soon left working on it alone, while I wandered off to use the restroom and then *accidentally* got distracted talking to my girlfriends in the kitchen while we snacked on a cheese from the charcuterie board the chef had left for us in the fridge. For about an hour, I wondered if he even noticed that I'd gone. When he came down soon after, he didn't say a thing. No recriminations, no questions.

He *did*, however, have a list of other activities for us he wanted to do that day. Just the two of us, so we could—and I quote—focus on our teamwork. Every single one of those activities required us to be fully clothed.

Honestly, it was starting to worry me.

Maybe he hadn't slept as well as I'd thought? I'd have to check and make sure he was getting a full eight hours—and maybe then some. Even if it took me spiking his hot chocolate with some antihistamine to get him to pass out. Dude was like the Energizer Bunny of husbands.

Because he had the energy to drag me out into a virtual snowstorm to "build a snow fort as a team." Adam had some experience with snow in his childhood, having grown up in northern Washington. But I was a desert-raised, southern California girl.

I wasn't meant to spend long periods of time in wet, slushy, *cold* snow. I was like Frosty the Snowman on a temperate day in Hawaii or the Wicked Witch of the West with a bucket of water over her head. Needless to say, I did the complete opposite of what I wanted from him in bed: I didn't last long. Once I got wet through my pants, my socks and my gloves, I was done for. No amount of coaxing or seeing how close we were to finishing our *elaborate palace* would get me to stay out there any longer.

Instead, I used the old bathroom excuse to escape and make a beeline for our room, where I peeled off the wet clothes and jumped in a hot shower to warm up. It took me five minutes under the spray to stop shivering. Then I picked out the warmest, fluffiest, fleece pajama pants and a sweatshirt and decided to fix us both spiked hot chocolate. Maybe a little liquor in his system would get him to calm down. *And* make him more suggestible. Since we had skiing on the schedule tomorrow, I wanted to spend some time today knocking boots.

He was out there almost another half hour before I cracked the window against the blizzard—okay, so maybe it had stopped snowing and there was just a little light yet very, very glacial—breeze. Again, Californian here.

"I made us some hot chocolate. Come in and sit with me by the fire. It'll taste great with Jenna's Bosnian cookies. We'll even *cuddle.*"

Jordan snickered loudly behind me. I shout-whispered at him to shut up over my shoulder before turning back to see Adam neck-deep in the slush, muttering that our "awesome project" wasn't finished yet.

By the time he did let go and give up, his hot chocolate had become chilled sludge.

And it was getting dark and almost time for us to go explore a nearby tourist attraction, Vallea Lumina—a unique forest light show. So much for spending alone time together. And so much for feeling his rough, masculine skin and muscles under my hands.

*Damn it.*

# CHAPTER 10
## *ADAM*

*BE SPONTANEOUS, THE LIST SAID. IT'LL BE FUN, THEY SAID.*

And before I'd been able to Google how to be spontaneous on my phone, I'd had to surrender it to the locker. And Emilia would kill me if she caught me breaking into the vault to bust it out.

I had to wing this one on my own.

Problem was, spontaneity was not in my wheelhouse. *At all.* No, I was the plotter and the planner. I had plans for my plans. And I had no idea if being spontaneous meant I wasn't allowed to plan our bout of spontaneity.

And besides, when would we have the chance? Each of the four couples and Heath had asked for a reprieve from the relentless itinerary. In addition, Dom Fischer wanted to have dinner with Mia and me.

I'd phoned him earlier in the day, pleasantly surprised that he was here. He was a part owner in the establishment, he'd told me, in much the same way that I had invested in the resort in St. Lucia where Emilia and I had married. But the most valuable part of the phone call had been the little tidbit he'd dropped to me about the existence of a natural hot spring within walking distance of our retreat.

We'd had fun taking private skiing lessons together that afternoon. It felt a bit like teamwork—working on a new skill together. I was satisfied that we'd ticked off that box. But as we returned that evening, all exhausted, my mind was on the next task in upping our marriage score.

I don't think I could take much more cuddling because it was making me horny as fuck, so I was calling that task done and moving on. Spontaneity. That was the one we were tackling tonight, come hell or high water—but good God, let's hope not.

After dinner, I coaxed Emilia outside on a walk with me, having promised enjoyment of the newly fallen snow. She'd eyed me suspiciously, not being a fan of the snow, or of cold in general. I might have promised her some great fun warming ourselves up afterward.

Damn, I was looking forward that.

It was an undeniably beautiful evening and even she was drawn further away, enjoying the sky full of stars ahead and the gleaming fresh powder that squeaked and crunched beneath our feet.

I just happened to steer us into the direction of where Dominic had told me the hot springs were. There, the white mountains in the distance glowed under the pale light of the quarter moon.

Emilia exclaimed with delight when she noticed the springs and we watched the steam rise and dissipate into the cold night air above the black, still pools. The air was tinged with a faintly acrid smell, like sulfur.

I turned to her and lowered the bomb. "Let's go for a swim."

Her brows shot up. "I don't have a suit on. Besides, it's too cold."

I bent and touched the water. "Feel how warm that water is." Then I pulled out the roll of towels that I'd tucked under my arm beneath my coat. "Besides, we don't need suits. I brought these. We can dry off and get dressed again when we're done."

Emilia bent toward me to inspect the towels. "Those… are kitchen towels."

I shrugged. "Who cares? They'll get us dry, won't they?"

She laughed. "They are like a foot and a half long…."

"Then we dry quickly and get back in our clothes. Come on… we are never spontaneous. Don't you want to just do something in the moment? Don't you just want to live a little and feel the excitement?"

Her jaw dropped, and she stared at me silently for a long moment. "Who are you, and what did you do with my husband?"

I'd heard that one before. All too recently.

Without another word, I shucked my clothes, laid them and the towels in a dry spot, and waded into the pool.

"It's so relaxing on the sore muscles from skiing." She rolled her eyes, clearly unconvinced.

"What are you doing?"

"I'm being spontaneous. And I want you to be spontaneous too. In fact, I'd find it a very big turn-on."

She froze. I leaned back into the water, the steam and heat closing around me. I wasn't lying. It felt fucking amazing. Just to lay it on a bit thicker, I let out a long sigh, watching my own breath fog out the screen of twinkling stars above.

She moaned and groaned and bitched a little bit. But in the end, she pulled off her clothes—while I thoroughly enjoyed the view. Then she heaped them on top of mine and joined me.

Yes. Now I had her right where I wanted her. Naked and warm. We were doing this. Spontaneity for the win.

That was another box ticked off the list, and we were that much closer to becoming the top-scoring married couple.

When she got within reach, I hooked my arms around her waist and pulled her to me. "Careful!" she exclaimed. "I had to tie my hair up with no elastic so it wouldn't get wet. I can't stomach the thought of walking back in in twenty-degree weather with wet hair."

"Let me distract you from that thought." I pulled her flush against me, suddenly feeling my lust come alive, surging through my bloodstream. Oh god, I really wanted to fuck her. Here. Now. And yes, it was so happening. And if she wasn't on board for that yet, she would be after I'd taken some time to convince her in all the best ways.

She melted against me then, and our mouths found each other. We shared a long, lingering kiss, deeply tasting each other. Her wet skin slid against mine, our legs lacing together erotically. Steam escaped our mouths every time they came apart. I was dizzy with the thought of having her here, more turned on than I'd been in a long time. Score one for spontaneity.

As a bonus, we were ticking another box off the list—a long make-out session. On the list, the making out wasn't supposed to lead to sex, but I was willing to bend that rule for the sake of my blue balls. The thought of having wet, steamy sex, right here, naked under the stars on a snowy evening was really doing it for me.

Emilia moaned against me and suddenly her legs cinched tightly around my hips. I was so hard I was aching and *really* wanted to fuck her as soon as possible. But in my rush to coax her into the pool, I'd forgotten to grab the damn condom from my coat pocket. Adam the planner. I'd planned so well, remembering to bring the condom with me and failed to grab it when I'd stripped off my clothes in ass-crack freezing weather. *Nice going, numb nuts.*

Right now, not-so-numb nuts, actually. They, and the rest of me, were feeling mighty fine considering the stunning woman who was currently wrapped around me. With my mouth still attached to hers, I eased us back over to the edge of the springs, toward the rock where we'd piled our clothes. We'd done this before, breaking off foreplay for the condom grab. So often, in fact, that it had become a regular part of our choreography. Emilia would touch and kiss me while I made the frantic search for the familiar foil packet.

If the situation was reversed, I'd do the same to her—torment her while she hunted down the condom. My favorite move was the hand-bra position, which she usually laughed and acted annoyed about, but I knew she secretly liked. I wished that my hands could always be her bra.

I broke away from her just long enough to flop my wet paw around, groping through our clothes for the elusive condom. Her hand had drifted southward and was now gripping me like a hand-jockstrap. Nice one, sweet wife...

Suddenly, off to the left, the bushes began to shake, branches snapping under a loud crashing sound. Emilia froze and tensed in my arms, eyes going wide.

"What is that?" she shout-whispered.

"Could be someone coming to jump in with us." I grimaced at her. Oh well, the best they'd see would be our bare asses as we pushed out of the hot spring, grabbed our shit and left.

The noise came again, a much louder crash. Emilia sucked in a gasp. "That was way too big to be a person."

I gulped, remembering the brief bit of research I'd done about the resort when she'd first proposed the idea to me. In this part of B.C. there was plenty of wildlife—some of it dangerous, like bears and moose.

Without another thought, I grabbed her around the arm. "C'mon, let's get the fuck out of here."

With a small shriek—for which I shushed her—we darted out of the hot spring. The frigid air slapped every cell on the surface of my skin, stinging like a swarm of wasps. Fuck, it was glacial out here.

I pushed that out of my mind, focused on Emilia's safety. I took her by the elbow and hauled her out of the water. Whatever-it-was continued to crash in the bushes less than a hundred yards away.

Emilia grabbed our clothes, and I grabbed the jackets and footwear. Then we booked it to another set of bushes just along the edge of the road. At this point, running through the neighborhood naked seemed more desirable than getting attacked by rabid wildlife.

Since we'd put some distance between us and the noise, I stopped her and we hastily shoved on some of our clothes. She pulled on her shirt and her jacket and, bottomless, stuffed her feet into her low boots. I pulled on my jeans and grabbed the rest of the shit while I shoved on my footwear. Fifteen seconds after leaving the pool, we were moving, hand in hand, down the lane back toward our secluded mansion.

And though I cocked an ear to see if it was following us, I never heard a thing. Emilia was bare-legged under her jacket—

which barely covered her ass. We were almost to the house when one of the private security cars for the gated community headed up the road in our direction. Shit. I grabbed my wife and pulled her into the side yard. That would be an awkward explanation to the rent-a-cops. And that was assuming they'd even believe us, instead of thinking we were some weird, half-naked cat-burglar Bonnie-and-Clyde team.

Despite my continued reminder for her to stay quiet, Emilia was rattling on in a loud but breathless whisper, as she shivered and pulled her tights over her wet legs. "Holy shit, that was totally a bear. It *had* to be a bear. Could you hear how big it was?"

I kept my eyes on the road, and again put my finger to my lips to silence her, while nodding to answer her question. When and if we made it in the front door, we'd look like a pair of drowned rats, but at least we were returning unmauled and with everything intact besides our dignity.

*Christ*, that had been a close call.

By the time we reached the front porch, our adrenaline had faded, and we were both legit shivering. And Emilia got cranky when she was cold, so I was motivated to get us inside lest I lose my chance for sex tonight.

But as soon as we busted through the door, my cousin, Liam, along with Jenna, Kat, Lucas and Heath all looked up from their Uno game.

"What happened? You look like you've seen a ghost," Jenna set down her cards and pushed up onto her knees to get a better look at us. Her eyes flicked to me and then back to my wife. "Maybe two ghosts."

Emilia pulled off her jacket. You'd never would have known she'd just pulled it on a minute before we'd open the door. She blew out a breathy laugh and hung up her coat "No, no... we walked up to the, um, up the road a bit—"

"To check out the view of the valley," I cut in case she planned on exposing our plot. Okay, poor choice of words, but yeah.

Liam frowned and opened his mouth. I just knew he was going to point out some inconsistency in our story, though we'd only rattled off two sentences between us. I plowed on before he could get a word out. "But we had a close call. Damn, it was scary. We were just standing there.... looking out at the view and—"

"Suddenly a bear was crashing through the bushes right toward us!" Emilia finished.

Lucas and Jenna's eyes grew huge with surprise and concern. Katya frowned and bit her lip and Liam, characteristically, scoffed. "There was no bear out there," he drawled.

"There was," I nodded vigorously, anxious to back up my wife's very accurate account. "It was huge, from the sound of it."

"But you didn't actually see it?" Heath asked.

"No, but there are bears all over this valley and the mountains. I read the place is crawling with them. There are even signs warning about bears on the side of the road. Bears definitely live here."

"True...." Kat said, her eyes flicking sideways, but Liam was shaking his head at me very decidedly. How the fuck would he know? It's not like he'd been to Canada before this. Ever.

"It was not a bear," my cousin refuted.

"Well, you weren't there, Mr. Know-it-all. So you have zero idea." I glared at him.

He looked at me like I was the biggest idiot he'd ever met. I was well familiar with that look. We had lived together in the same house as teens. "I know it wasn't a bear because of the date."

"The date?" Emilia cocked her head. "What do you mean?"

"It's late December, almost January. Adam is right. There are probably thousands of bears living in this area. But none of them was out there in your bushes with you while you were... doing whatever you were doing. Every single bear around here is hibernating right now."

Oh, huh. Shit. He was right.

"Well then it was definitely a moose. A huge ass bull moose."

Kat bit her lip and looked decidedly like she was about to contradict me. "Have you ever seen a moose in person? Like close? They are six to eight feet tall at the shoulder. I don't think they could hide in a bush unless it was a pretty damn huge bush."

"Trust the Canadian to know the true moose facts," snarked her husband, which earned him a playful punch in his bicep.

Emilia scanned them all, from William to Kat and back. "Well then, what the hell was it? It was way too big to be a dog or a raccoon."

Kat grimaced, as if hesitant to embarrass her friend. "My guess? It was most likely a whitetail deer."

Emilia turned to me and I turned to her. We held gazes for a long moment. No one said a word. The silence was deafening. Almost as if on cue, we both bust up laughing.

"Whoops. I guess the big bad deer almost caught us in the buff!" Mia snickered after we calmed down.

"In the buff?" Kat piped up with widened eyes. "*What?*"

My bride immediately blushed crimson, biting her lip and sending me an *oh crap* look.

"Just an expression." I jerked my chin toward the stairs and she nodded, trotting up them before we said anything more to incriminate ourselves.

"Mia, your leggings are on inside-out!" Jenna called in a sing-song voice before we disappeared from their view. The response was quiet chuckles from the rest of the group. *Busted.*

When we got to our room, Mia was frantically looking for her hat and scarf.

"I might have dropped along the way, damn it! I don't want to go back down there after all that..."

"I'm on it." I gave her a long hug. "Go take a hot shower and get in bed. I'll go have a look."

I walked all the way back to the springs—this time with a flashlight I'd found by the front door. On the way back, toward the side yard where we'd dashed, I found the lost items.

When I got back, the card game had broken up and most of the people were no longer there. I was starving, so I headed for the kitchen to grab a snack. Jordan was in there fixing himself a sandwich.

"Hey man, heard you had some excitement tonight," he said with a waggle of his brows.

Oh jeez. Now everyone knew?

I clenched my jaw. "We won't speak of it."

"*You* might not speak of it, but damn if I'm not going to have a lot of fun speaking of it."

Time to change the subject. I walked over to the bowl on the counter, plucked a banana and peeled it.

"So how're the plans for Operation Big Rock going?"

Jordan stiffened and made frantic hand waving motions with his hands while glancing over his shoulder.

"That good?" I grinned between bites of my banana.

"The concierge is headed over any minute, so we can talk about it. I need ideas."

I glanced at the clock and raised my brows. "Wow, I thought Emilia was exaggerating. She really *is* into you."

Jordan shook his head. "Naw. But the assistant is coming along too, and it's pretty obvious that he wants in Heath's pants."

I almost chocked on my banana. I didn't know too much about Heath's specific preferences but it didn't take a rocket scientist to know that Anna's thin, very young, and mildly effeminate assistant, while a very nice guy, was nowhere even close to the type of guys Heath normally went for.

"That's not going to go over well," I muttered, discarding the banana peel into the compost pail.

"What, the proposal or fixing those two up?" Jordan said in a low whisper.

"Fixing them up. But I wish you good luck with the rest of it, man. Don't ask me for any creative ideas because I'm hard-pressed to come up with any of my own these days." I slapped him on the shoulder. "I'm out. Good night."

When I finally made it back to our room, Emilia was fast asleep. I took my own turn at a nice hot shower and collapsed into bed. As I wrapped myself around her prone form, I had to admit to a little amount of relief.

I'd jump her bones in the morning.

# CHAPTER 11
## JORDAN

I HAD TO OFFLOAD THIS RING AS SOON AS POSSIBLE. I'D managed to stash it at the very back of my underwear and sock drawer. In fact, I'd actually tucked it inside a roll of socks so that it would be hard to detect even if she did open up the drawer for whatever reason.

But damn, until I figured out how I was going to do the proposal, that thing was going to hang like an albatross around my neck. I'd been in constant fear of her discovering it. The box was a little big—being a work of intricate engineering wizardry. It lit up when you opened it.

Yeah I was *that* sucker who'd paid extra for the fucking box that lit up and shone a light on the diamond when the box opened. I pictured her gazing down at the gleaming stone and being bedazzled, even as I was down on one knee trying not to hyperventilate at the thought of what I was doing.

In reality, this very expensive hardware wouldn't make any big difference in our relationship. We'd already been living as committed, monogamous live-in partners. We could just end up being eternally engaged. Who gave a crap about a wedding? A marriage? Just a piece of paper, really. We could talk all that out once I got the damn ring on her finger, provided I hadn't keeled over from hyperventilation in the process.

Anna, the snow bunny concierge, finally tapped on the back door and I let her in with a finger across my lips. Though it was after ten at night, she was freshly made up and dressed to the nines in a form-fitting jumpsuit. When she smiled wide, I almost had to squint from the glare. Too many teeth in that mouth or something….

Whatever, she was here to help me figure this out. It was her job, after all. Anna's assistant quickly scanned the kitchen, and then, without a word to either his boss or me, he disappeared into the living room, no doubt on the hunt for Heath. I felt for Heath, all too familiar with the clingy types that didn't get the hint—or thousand—when you weren't interested.

Heath was a big boy and could handle rejecting a puppy himself. I had bigger fish to fry, at the moment.

"Hey there, Jordan," Anna purred, beaming up at me as she set down a very fancy-looking sticker-covered planner on the kitchen counter. "I'm happy to help with whatever your event is. Just waiting to get the details…" Her eyelashes fluttered and that too-wide smile widened even more.

Whatever.

"I'm more than willing to make it worth your while for the extra work. But yes, I have something very important I'd like you to handle."

Oh shit, that didn't come out right. Her cheeks flushed a little and there was a suggestive look in her eye.

Anna's thin eyebrows arched almost to the brim of her little knit snow-bunny hat. She flicked her wavy blond hair over her shoulder and laughed. "It's my job to make you happy."

I blinked. Subtle she was not. I guess Adam was right about this chick after all. *Ugh.*

Who cared? The minute I let her in on what I wanted her to do, she'd get a clue and stop hitting on me. I wasn't even the least bit tempted. A man doesn't go out for hamburgers when he's getting perfectly prepared Prime Rib at home every night, every morning and sometimes at noon. *Nope.*

"See, I have a ring for my girlfriend. You met April, right? I want to propose to her while we're up here, but I need it to be an epic moment. Can you help me out with that?"

She glanced off to the side, appearing annoyed and then shrugged a shoulder. "Sure. We've helped out with things like that before. The ski lodge has some lovely overlooks. Or up on the slope..."

I stiffened, shaking my head. "That's nice, but I want something...." I gestured big with my hands. "Truly out of the ordinary. Think *epic.*"

Anna angled her head at me, bending slightly to give me a full view of her cleavage. I was familiar with that maneuver. Whatever. I looked away. "Uh, are you sure?"

I scowled at her. "Sure about what? Of course, I'm sure. Why would you ask that?"

Her eyes widened, lashes batting furiously, and she drew back sharply. "Oh, oh, I'm sorry I just mean are you sure you don't want to do it on a high slope or on the peak by the Inukshuk?"

"The what-a-what?"

"Oh, it's that First Nations-style monument up on the peak? You know, I pointed it out to you the first morning you were here? A lot of proposals have been done there. We can set it up, get some fur wraps to keep her warm and—"

I shook my head. "No. Bigger. I want this to be the proposal that she can't stop bragging to her friends about. Not only that, I want people here telling the story of the epic proposal. Can you be a bit more creative?"

Anna stared at me open-mouthed, batting her lashes, as if her brain didn't really work that fast, and she was still processing what I'd said to her ten minutes ago.

From around the corner, her assistant—Jonny? Joey?—piped in. "What about the Peak 2 Peak, Anna? Like...we could get them on one by themselves. He could ask her there as they cross over the valley."

I shook my head. "Peak 2 Peak? What's that?"

"It's a gondola," Anna said with a decidedly unexcited tone to her voice. "It travels between Blackcomb Peak and Whistler Mountain. And if you want epic, it is the tallest and longest gondola ride on the continent."

I nodded, considering. "Okay so we just...ride in this thing and I ask her as we ride? How long is the ride?"

Jed—no Joe—oh, whatever his name was, smiled big. "Twenty-two minutes from station to station. But you could loop around, if you want to double that."

I waved my hand in a circle, motioning. "Okay but...while we're in there that long, what are we doing? Besides taking in the view or just chatting, I mean."

"Drinks? Appetizers?" The assistant pitched to Anna.

"How about a three-course meal while we're at it?" Anna snorted, teasing her assistant, but that actually sounded like a great idea.

"Yeah, let's do that. We can loop around three times, right? Twenty-two minutes for each course seems about right?"

"I'll make a note to check on availability first thing in the morning," the assistant chimed in as Anna's face darkened.

"Damn. Phone's dead. I need some paper... paper... I'll go ask Heath if he has a pad in his room."

As he disappeared around the corner, I called after him, "There's a pad here on the fridge."

No answer.

Obviously, the paper wasn't the only thing he wanted. Heath had probably bolted by now.

Anna sidled up to me, twisting a strand of her blond hair around her index finger and biting her lip like a Playboy playmate. "Uhh, we've never done anything like this before. Tying up the gondola for an hour and a half? Setting up a dinner in there? It's, ah, never been done."

I smiled. "All the better reason to do it, then. Seems pretty epic to me. Perfect!"

"What's perfect?" a voice called from the doorway. We all turned to look. April stood in her silky kimono and slippers, an empty water bottle in her hand. Her keen eyes flicked from Anna, who was standing way too close to me, then to me and back again.

"Uh, nothing, uh, I mean..." I fumbled. Shit. Here I thought I'd be safe talking about this in the kitchen. I thought April had already crashed.

"Oh, I just had a few questions regarding the schedule. I thought Jordan might have some answers so that I can better see to everyone's...needs." Her smile toward my girlfriend was sickly sweet. I recognized the reaction in April's deep blue eyes. Her hackles were up.

Well maybe her being a little jealous was a good thing. A good red herring to follow for a little while to keep her from discovering the truth.

April moved into the room and stood beside me. I startled when she put her hand firmly on my ass and squeezed. "Are we all done here? Because I have some needs that need seeing to." She stared up at me, her deep blue eyes burning with... something. Passion or anger? I couldn't tell.

Hopefully those needs would involve me dropping trou and April on her knees in front of me.

Thankfully, Anna and what's-his-name showed themselves out shortly thereafter with a quietly worded promise that she'd text me the minute she had any news.

# Chapter 12
## *April*

Holy crap, who the hell did this chick think she was? What a… my mind raced. Had I any internalized misogyny going on inside my psyche, I may have already deemed her a THOT. But I didn't roll like that. *I* had integrity.

But no one blatantly flirted with my man and got away with it. This woman did *not* want to mess with me. My *oma* had taught me some good curses from the old world, and this Anna woman had no evil eye to shield her. Screw this shit.

Next time I saw her, I'd definitely be pulling her aside and let her know she was treading on thin ice and I knew what she was up to. It was a certainty that in her job, she met tons of rich guys. And it might be rare to find one this young, cut, and devastatingly handsome. Jordan was a rare find. But he was mine.

Back in our room, sexy times before bed were in order. Time to get Jordan's head back in my game—so to speak. The minute we were inside our room and the door shut, I didn't hesitate. I was all over him like cheap spandex leggings. My hand on his crotch, I went up on tiptoes and started mouthing his neck.

"I need you," I whispered. "*Now.*"

Under my hand, he hardened immediately. He bent to cover my mouth with his. His breathing quickened and his hands roamed all over my body. *That's a good Beast.*

Jordan's hands cupped my shoulders, directed me toward the bed, but when we got there, instead of getting on the bed, I went for his belt buckle instead. His eyes darkened with understanding. My hand moved over the zipper, pulling it down with some difficulty. These jeans fit snugly, and even snugger when he was fully erect. But soon I returned from that treasure hunt with my prize in hand. My hot, rigid prize. *Mouthwatering.*

I raised my chin to meet his gaze, then slowly sank to my knees, holding his eyes with mine while I licked my lips. He froze, holding his breath. When I plunged him into my mouth, he threw his head back with a groan. "Fuck," he rasped. A hand reached out to brace himself on the bedpost.

I loved giving him head and he loved receiving, naturally. He wasn't obnoxious but sometimes, when he got caught up in it, he'd grab my hair and take control, push me where he wanted me to go, thrust himself deep and talk dirty to me the entire time he did it. Sexy, *sexy* Beast.

I was only getting started, tantalizing and tormenting him with my tongue while he surged inside my mouth, breath coming raggedly. Just as he was reaching for my hair, however, his phone rang. His hand froze, but I didn't stop. He could ignore his fuckin' phone for God's sake. He was getting a first-class, top-notch BJ. And my Beast rarely let anything interrupt sex.

The phone kept ringing. He pulled it out of his pocket to turn it off. Except no, he didn't turn it off. What the fuck? He put his hand on my head... to pull himself away with a slight gasp. Then he stepped back and answered the phone. Was this really happening right now?

I froze, still kneeling on the ground, while he retreated to the other side of the room by the windows, the phone to his ear. "Yeah," he said without even looking in my direction. This had better be something vital and urgent at work or this was some bullshit. Especially at this hour. "Uh huh. Okay. Yes, that sounds good if you can work that all out. Ah—yeah. I think I can. I'll, yeah. Get back to you."

His voice sounded weird... like tight, like he was a little stressed out. Or a lot stressed out. I slumped over to the bed and pulled myself onto it. He tossed the phone onto the bed and proceeded to button up. Even weirder. Not that I was inclined to continue now, but I was shocked that he wasn't going to come back over here and at least try, so I could decently reject him. What the....what?

He was really weirding me out.

"We should turn in, babe. I'm exhausted and I need to be up early tomorrow. Guys thing. I'll probably be gone when you wake up."

I blinked. My mouth opened and closed a few times. I didn't remember seeing anything like that on the itinerary. Was it an impromptu thing? Maybe they were going to work out or something?

He wasn't even meeting my gaze to take in my shocked expression. "I'm gonna go take a shower now so I don't wake you up. Do you need anything? Oh right, you came into the kitchen to get more water, didn't you? Let me go get you that. Be right back." He left the room and I sat, running fingers through my hair, mind racing for what to do and wishing Mia was awake so I could ask her advice.

He returned in minutes, setting not one, but two chilled water bottles on my nightstand. Then he kissed the top of my head.

"Go to bed, babe. You look tired." I glared at his receding back as he headed for the bathroom. *Thanks a lot, asshole.*

I flopped back on the bed, staring at the ceiling and wondering what to do as I listened to the water turn on in the bathroom.

Suddenly, his phone lit up right beside me, buzzing with a text. I scooped it up before the message faded from the update screen.

Anna: *Give me a call in the morning when you're up and about and we'll make plans to meet. I've already got a list of ideas for us.*

My eyelashes fluttered so quickly they probably resembled hummingbird wings. How? What? My gut tightened and a sick miasma began churning in my stomach. How was this possible? Was my Beast cheating? Or trying to get away in order to think about doing it? Or?

What the hell even was this?

Because of his past, I never in a zillion years would suspect him of straying. *Ever.*

I knew down to my bones that if he ever wanted out of the relationship, he'd come to me and tell me so before moving on to some other woman's bed.

But here was proof that not only did he have her number, he was actively planning to meet with her for...for what?

Then another realization pounded down on my head so hard it threatened to sicken me. Had that been her on the phone? Had he actually interrupted oral sex with me to talk to *her*?

How weirdly ironic that our own secret affair, back when ours was a forbidden boss-assistant fling, had started nearby in the city of Vancouver, just an hour south of where we were right now. *What happens in Canada stays in Canada,* he'd joked then. *Ugh.* Was that still the case for him? Did he still see Canada as some tomcat free-for-all land of milk and honey-bunnies?

I set his phone on the nightstand and rubbed my temples. I couldn't handle this right now. I needed ice cream—and someone to talk to. Tightening my kimono belt, I put my slippers back on and headed out of the room. I was too wound up to sleep, and it was way too late and crowded in this house for me to confront him now.

I needed to cool down. I needed a level head. I needed my girls.

I could barely suck in a shaky breath. What the hell was this? How could we have gone from doing so amazingly well to his eye very obviously roving in just a few days in the country? Had I pushed it too much with all my teasing and playacting about wanting to get married? It had all been in fun. He'd known that. He had to know that.

I wasn't ready to get married. But playing on his obvious aversion to it had always been worth a few laughs, particularly with the girls. It had been my fun way of just connecting and flirting with him and letting him know that I knew he was mine even if we weren't official.

He *knew* that.

I mean... right? He did know that, right? How could he not know that?

My mind played through some of the things I done for a laugh—openly ogling Mia's wedding gown; looking at Bride magazines when Sid dumped them on me with her not-so-subtle hints; *oooh*ing and *aaah*ing over Kat's antique art deco engagement ring.

It had *all* been to get his goat.

Oh damn, April, you really blew it now didn't you? *You idiot.*

Everyone had gone to bed, besides Heath, who was on the PlayStation playing some game that looked like soccer but with cars. We didn't talk, since he had the headset on to keep the game quiet, and I was fine with that.

I had a half quart of mint chocolate chip ice cream and a large soup spoon in my hand and I was not afraid to use them. Hours later, when I finally made it back to our room, Jordan was dead to the world.

And by the time I finally drifted off, and woke up late in the morning, he was long gone.

When I checked my phone, I was reminded that this morning, just a half hour from now, was girls' brunch and in-house spa day.

My girls. I needed them. The timing couldn't be better.

A short time later we were in our swimsuits in the bubbling jacuzzi that sat on the covered sundeck—labeled the *solarium*—beside a small infrared sauna and a few gym machines. This place never ceased to amaze me. We had everything here.

The girls were all chatting happily, sharing stories, but I heard none of it. I sipped absently at my mimosa and stared out at the mountain view, deep in thought. I was a zillion miles away when I realized all the girls were staring at me.

"Hmm, what?"

"What's going on with you, April? You seem super distracted," Jenna asked. "Everything okay?"

I blinked and frowned. Well, I couldn't exactly bring up what was on my mind, could I? But they might have some good advice for me. I nibbled at my bottom lip. What to do… what to do…

Hmm. When all else failed… lie.

"Hmm oh sorry, I was just thinking about my good friend… Sid."

"Oh, your former roommate?" Mia asked.

I blinked. Oh shit. Yeah I'd forgotten that Mia and met Sid once. Since Sid had graduated and taken a job up in LA, we didn't see each other very often these days, but she didn't have a boyfriend. It was probably safe to use her for my lie.

Of course, with my luck, we'd probably end up crossing paths with her up here. Or at LAX on the way home, or something.

"Yeah…so. Sid's seeing this guy. They've been together for a while now. And she, um, she thinks he might be cheating. Or planning to cheat on her."

I swallowed, scanning each of their faces. Could they tell I was lying like a rug? I was literally doing that "asking for a friend" thing. Well, in for a Guess bag, in for a Louis Vuitton….

"Oh, poor Sid," Jenna said. "She must be so stressed out."

I nodded. "She is. Sick to her stomach, too."

Mia leaned forward and patted my shoulder. "So, she just suspects it, right? She's not sure?"

I cocked my head, avoiding Mia's eyes. "She was asking me for advice. Didn't know what to say."

"You should tell her to sit him down and ask him directly what's going on," Mia said.

I nodded. "That sounds like good advice. I'll pass that along"

Jenna shook her head, staring out the window. "I could not abide a cheater. Or even one who flirts with women while he's in a relationship."

"Well, I think it's more that the other chick is flirting a lot with Sid's boyfriend." Shit I should probably think up a name for this fictional guy soon or they'd be on to me. Carl? Jimmy? No... um. Harold? Jaden?

"Some other chick is trying to swoop in and get her man? Uh uh." said Kat with a final, chopping gesture. "Burn it all down. Tell Sid to take up some martial arts and learn how to throw a right hook. Or just use something heavy and—"

Jenna held out a hand to interrupt Kat mid-gesture. "Now, now. Sometimes we just need to follow John Lennon's advice and give peace a chance. Talking. In the end, it's all about Sid and the trust between her and her boyfriend....What's his name?"

"Ro—ca, Um, Roland." I sputtered. Shit, almost gave myself up there. Last minute save. Roland? WTF? Was he a medieval Knight of the Round Table or something?

"Well as much as I'd be tempted to Kat's route, I agree with Jenna." Mia said with a decisive nod. "This is a him and her situation. The flirty woman can't cheat unless he allows it to happen."

My guts sank and my throat tightened and I nodded miserably before tilting the champagne flute back to get every single last drop. Kat already had the bottle poised to refill it when I came up for air.

If Jordan was cheating—or planning to cheat—would he tell me, even if I asked him to his face?

I vowed to get to the bottom of it tonight. We were supposed to have dinner alone together. I had no details on where or when or how. But the sooner I did it, the better.

Because I don't think I could invent more friends to ask for still more advice. And I was already feeling buzzed at eleven thirty in the morning. My mind raced for a way to change the subject. Fortunately, Mia did it for me.

"Oh, by the way, April, remember that mystery man who came to the door and gave me his card? I have news."

Now we were talking. I was immediately pulled out of my sulk by the promise of juicy gossip. With a deep breath, I shoved all thoughts of my current dilemma to the background and vowed I wouldn't obsess about it again until I was alone.

"Spill the tea, girl. I need to know everything!"

# CHAPTER 13
## *JENNA*

WAIT, WHAT WAS THIS? I BLINKED, SETTING DOWN my own flute of champagne to follow the excited chatter of my friends. Just when I was going to ask for my own advice, too…

Kat frowned, as lost as I was. "Who are you guys talking about?"

April gestured excitedly. "Oh, this guy came to the door yesterday. He was… *exceptional.* I mean, we have a lot of fantastic eye-candy here in the house. And we love our guys, but—"

"Fresh meat?" Kat said with a hearty giggle. "A girl can still look, right?"

April quirked a smile. "What's hilarious is that I punched his name into Google right after he left to find out more about him, and then got distracted before I could even read up on what I'd found. So…" She nodded expectantly at Mia. "Fill us in!"

"Well Adam knows him from his time when he worked at Sony, pre-Draco. His name is Dom Fischer and he now also runs his own company."

April's forehead wrinkled. "He seemed a bit older than Adam, though. Like in his thirties."

Mia laughed. "Adam's turning thirty in just a few months."

General admission all around about how old that seemed. I was still several years away from that milestone myself, thank goddess!

"Just how many billionaire BFFs does Adam have tucked away in his back pocket, and why didn't I know this when I was single?" Kat snorted.

April tilted her head. "So he runs a gaming company too? A competing company to Draco?"

Mia waved her hand airily. "Oh no, he's not in games anymore. His business is autonomous cars. Apparently, it just blew up with some new product they put out on the market—vehicles without drivers that deliver goods and food to customers' homes."

April's eyes bugged out. "Are you talking about Tranxit? We've been talking about them in my MBA program. Jeez, now I know why he looks so familiar..."

Mia reached over and topped off April's glass. "Apparently the story is, when he left Sony, he tried to hire Adam to work for him. But Adam was already on his way out to start his own company. As we all probably could surmise, my hubby doesn't like working for other people."

Kat snorted. "Understatement of the year."

"That's saying a lot when there's only a few more days left in the year, too." Mia took a last sip of champagne before setting it aside on the ledge of the jacuzzi.

April was frowning as if trying to remember something. "He had some big, publicized split with his girlfriend and a lawsuit. Some semi-famous model. It was all tabloid-worthy, of course."

"Aren't they always models?" I shook my head. I'd say guys like that don't date any other type, but here I was, sitting with two friends who were the significant others of billionaires, so I kept my mouth shut and finished off my mimosa.

Mia's gaze flicked to April. "He had a really intimidating vibe to him. Like a cross between a stern daddy and an enforcer. Even his name implies it—*Dom*. Was it domestic violence or something?"

April shook her head. "No. Libel, I'm pretty sure. She tried to get some trashy tell-all memoir about their relationship published, and he filed an injunction to block it."

"Who are you guys even talking about? I'm lost." I looked from one of them to the other.

Kat had already picked up her phone and was typing into it. "I had the same questions, so I just searched him and… whoa. I think he'd be fine getting models even if he was a penniless desk jockey."

She flipped the phone so that I could see the pictures she'd pulled up. I paged through the first three, stopping at the shirtless one, obviously a pap photo snapped at the beach. He wore tight European-style swim trunks and had an ah-mazing body. Thick, dark hair, silvery gray eyes. Holy moly. Think all the hot Chris actors—Evans, Pine, Hemsworth and Pratt—rolled in to one, with the poise and presence of Idris Elba, or Pedro Pascal. Add in a dash of Theo James.

It's a wonder the phone wasn't melting in Kat's hand. That was a lot of hotness to handle.

"*That's* the self-driving car tech nerd?" I asked with a slight gasp.

"Yup," Kat answered. "But, like, I'm a happily married lady, so my panties totally aren't melting right now. If they're a bit warm, it's because of the jacuzzi. We should figure out which of our friends to throw at him."

"Maybe April's friend, Sid," I suggested helpfully. "Help her move on from possibly-cheating guy."

April's features clouded. She definitely didn't like that idea.

"If I didn't know about the story with the ex-girlfriend and the memoir, I'd say he could be gay, since the uber-hot ones usually are." Kat smirked as she set her phone aside. "So why's the memoir so bad? Is it about the sex stuff he's into? Like kinky stuff or whatever?"

April shook her head. She was always good for the famous people gossip. "Everyone's speculating. Especially since Tranxit landed that huge government contract. The lawsuit is still tied up in the courts. Honestly, if he didn't get her to sign an NDA before they hooked up, then he's a dummy. Of course, there are all kinds of rumors flying around that she's going to spill about how he's into orgies and kink. And since he looks the way he does, some are calling him a 'real-life Christian Grey.'"

"For the kind of money he's worth, I might consider a few handcuffs and a riding crop," Kat cut in with a snort. "He's Adam's friend. What tea did your hubby spill to you about him?"

Mia's mouth twisted. "Very little. Guys don't talk to each other about that kind of stuff. I doubt Adam knows anything at all about his private life, nor does he care. Dudes are frustratingly uncurious about their peers." We all laughed at that. "Honestly, he seems very warm to Adam, and to me by extension, but there's something there that's a little scary."

April nodded. "I'd say intimidating, but yeah, he had that kind of presence for sure."

I cocked my head. "Like, do you think he's toxic?"

"You girls are overthinking it. Guys like that are probably great if you just want a fun, enjoyable shag." Kat held up her flute for a refill on her champagne. "Maybe my hubby's aristocrat influence is wearing off on me, but I used to fucking hate champagne with a red hot bloody passion. This stuff isn't bad."

The talk dissipated into other things and I zoned out again, back into my head. I watched Kat absently as she sipped her champagne, thinking about what Lucas had told me our first day here—that he made it a conscious habit to tell her he loved her every night as the last thing he said to her. That had left such an impression on me that I hadn't truly stopped thinking about it.

What were William's feelings? He was so hard to read. But he'd totally be the type of man to stay with someone, even if he didn't love them anymore—out of a sense of loyalty and honor.

Before I even realized I was talking, I blurted out my question to the group. "How often do your guys verbally tell you that they love you? I mean, using those exact words?"

My friends all glanced at each other and then at me. "Uh, I don't really count." April says.

"I don't mean the precise number." I blew out a breath of frustration. "I'm just talking...in general. How often?"

Mia shrugged, stretching her arms across the lip of the jacuzzi behind her. "Couple times a week, I'd say. Sometimes in person, sometimes in text."

"Pretty much every time we hook up," April said with a sly grin.

Kat laughed at both of her friends. "I get it fairly often. But it doesn't count when he's grumpy, so that takes a bunch of them away."

We all laughed at that, but I sobered quickly, biting my lip. When I looked up, I noticed all eyes on me. I blinked.

"Is he not saying it to you?" Mia asked.

I shrugged. "Well, you know Wil. He's not a big talker." I gulped and suddenly wished for the champagne flute back, just for something to do.

Mia bit her lip. "He isn't. But he absolutely does love you, you know, even if he doesn't say it as often as you'd like. Maybe just talk to him about it?"

I sighed. Just talk to him about it. I guess that was an option. But it might bring on an argument, which I didn't want, or make him defensive or think less of himself. Or—good god—what if he just blurted out that he didn't?

Ugh. My stomach twisted.

"It's probably just sexual frustration. Seduce him," Heath advised me in the reading nook later that day. I'd been sitting there knitting on the scarf-that-would-never-end and staring at the mountains in quiet contemplation, hoping to bring some inner peace.

Heath and I had gotten to talking a little, and *this* was his advice… How unoriginal for a guy to suggest sex as the cure-all for every problem.

That definitely wasn't our issue. William and I had a very healthy and fulfilling sex life. But I didn't bother to disavow Heath of that assumption. I respected Wil's preference for privacy, after all. Then again, I'd already asked several people about how to deal with the *I love you* situation.

"William's constantly hunched over that sketch book. I've been watching him." Kat said later during an outdoor walk to stretch our legs—after William had declined my invitation.

We made it down the lane to the natural hot springs nearby. But only a crazy person would go swimming in this weather. No matter that the water was probably warm, the air definitely was *not.* Kat tested the water with her finger, then pulled it out, shaking it off, declaring it way too hot. Guess we'd stick to the indoor jacuzzi, then.

"He told me the sketching is some kind of special project he's working on. I know it's not for work, because even Adam noticed and asked him if he was doing work, but he said no. I don't know...maybe his muse has struck him."

We turned to go back the way we'd come. "But aren't *you* his muse?"

I shrugged. These days, I didn't feel like it. We got back to the mansion shortly before lunch was ready. I actually grabbed the sketch pad when he left the room to use the bathroom. I shoved it down the back cushion of the same chair he'd been sitting in. *There.* Now he'd have to pay attention to me!

But it took less than three minutes of my conscience eating at me to chicken out. He'd exited the bathroom and headed straight into the kitchen—briefly stopping to ask if I wanted him to bring me something to drink. As soon as he vanished into the kitchen, I hurriedly removed the pad from its hiding place and replaced it where he'd left it minutes before.

I just couldn't bring myself to do it. But I sure would have liked it better if he didn't go back to the sketch pad right after lunch, which he did. So I sat beside him and did my *flawed* knitting instead. Almost done. When it was a scarf, I'd wrap it around his neck and insist we spend some time in the great outdoors.

The best suggestion came from April as we were getting ready for our afternoon activity, a wine and cheese tasting at the local, high-end restaurant.

"I have an idea. You should do something fun and romantic that will force him to hold your hand the whole time."

"And what would that be?" I braced myself for another sex suggestion like Heath's.

"Go ice skating!"

I all but laughed. Goddess, what a brilliant idea!

# CHAPTER 14
## *WILLIAM*

I DON'T LIKE ICE SKATING. AND I *REALLY* DON'T LIKE BEING out in the cold much. My cheeks sting. And it's really disconcerting that I can see exactly how much breath I exhale every single time. I don't like being able to see air. It's not natural. I point this out to Jenna as we make our way to the rink in the little village of Whistler. But all she does is laugh.

She must think I'm joking. She should know better by now. I most definitely am *not* joking.

But here we are, putting on ice skates—*rented* ice skates that have recently been worn by someone else. "There are more than two hundred different types of fungi that inhabit the human foot," I mutter as I pull the boot on.

"That's why they spray them out with cleaner in between every use. Plus, people do have socks on."

"I'm not convinced that they do an adequate job with coverage to get every spot."

She bends over me to help tighten my laces, her hair falling forward and exposing her long, pale neck. Every time I see that neck exposed, I want to kiss it. Every time. Most of those times I refrain.

The boot leather closes around my ankles and I suppress a wince. New experiences. We'd agreed...both of us...that we'd try anything once—within reason. At the beginning of our relationship, we'd sat down and had this discussion. I could hard pass on up to ten types of activities—anything involving heights, for example, was on the no list. But she could count on me to have an open mind to try things at least once. I could then declare that something we did that I don't like would go on a *never do again* list. The water park and mud spa are at the top of *that* list.

After tightening my laces, Jenna stands up, then pulls something out of the plastic shopping bag she'd carried with her. It's the beige wool scarf she's been knitting for me. My specially-made-by-hand Christmas present. She'd purchased some things for me too, new shirts, socks, a few art journals, a fountain pen and ink, and some fresh new chalk pastels—the brand I preferred. But the scarf, a product of her hands, is what I've truly treasured.

Now she's wrapping it around my neck. It's a little scratchy on my cheeks. I don't like natural wool against my skin, but this type was softened with lanolin. It's more tolerable, and my cheeks don't sting as much with the cold now. Besides, I love the way she looks as she meticulously arranges it and ties it around my neck. I look up at her, studying her face as she concentrates on what she's doing. She's wearing pale pink, which is the color I've always preferred seeing on her. It blends well with her coloring, that pale blond-white hair, those cerulean eyes.

Beautiful. Breath-taking. In fact, I'm holding my breath right now as I look at her. On her head, a pale pink knit beanie is pulled down past her ears, her long silky hair spilling out over her shoulders. She's exquisite. And she's mine.

And she spent hours practicing how to knit while making this scarf just for me. It's far from perfect, as I've pointed out to her.

And with practice, she'll improve. But this scarf is precious. Even if a little scratchy.

No matter.... time to venture out on the ice with all of my body weight balanced on top of two thin blades. This looks so much easier watching it on the screen at the Olympics.

"I learned how to skate when I was a little girl in Bosnia." She said, wrapping her hand around mine. She suddenly looks so much smaller now that I'm standing, looking down at her. "My papa loved skating, so he took us out into the country and we'd skate on a crystal clear frozen lake. Every time I go ice skating, I remember those days."

A sweet memory. I'd be more charmed about it if I wasn't currently scared for my own life. As we hit the entrance to the rink, my heart is beating, and my breath—oh so visible with every puff—is streaming everywhere. All the more annoying. I'm so distracted by my heavy breathing fogging up the surrounding air that I barely register the minute my blades hit the ice. And I almost go flying.

*Nope. Nope.* Okay. I've tried it. I don't like—as predicted—and now I'm done. Time to add another entry to the list.

"Move to the railing, Will! Use it to steady yourself."

I do as she asks, shuffling awkwardly over to the edge.

"I'm going to break my skull on that ice." I nod toward the ice to emphasize where it just might happen.

"You're not going to break your skull. I'm right here."

I study her feet. She's standing confidently on her blades as if she's lived on them her entire life. I frown. Not fun. Not fun at all. I am officially not having fun, nor have I had fun since slipping the borrowed boots of questionable cleanliness onto my feet.

I'm still clinging to the railing unmoving like it's my lifeline. "I'd like to point out that my body weight and overall strength is almost one and a half times yours, so I fail to see how you'd prevent me from falling and breaking my skull."

A burst of foggy air escapes Jenna's mouth, and she looks like she's trying hard not to laugh. "I could cushion you if you fall. You could fall on me."

I give her a look. "I'd rather crush my own skull than injure you."

"You aren't going to do either. C'mon Wil, one time around the rink and you'll be on your own two feet like a pro. I bet you'll love it enough to go around more times!"

She's wrong. I don't like it one bit, and it takes us nearly three quarters of an hour to make it around to the point where we started. She isn't smiling as much now.

"I'm cold and this fog is making it hard to see," I tell her.

"Yes, yes. I got that the fifth time you told me." She sounds weary now—tired and not her sparkling self. She keeps wanting to hold hands as I shuffle slowly along but I don't trust that. I have both hands hooked on the railing, making progress by inches. The end is almost in sight.

Happily, I make it and spend the rest of the session sitting in the stand sipping hot chocolate while I watch her skate easily against the backdrop of the pale mountains all around us. She can do turns and even skate backwards. Watching her is much more fun than attempting that circuit on those death blades.

My eyes are still watering from the cold, but my hands are warm, thanks to the cocoa. My cheeks are warm thanks to her imperfect, scratchy wool scarf. This isn't ideal, but it's much better than risking my life on the ice. Plus, I get to watch my beautiful girl glide across the ice, a childlike smile on her face. It brings to mind another black ink and watercolor I'd like to do. But I've got that very important project to finish first. Unfortunately, the sketchbook is back at the cabin. I make plans to get to it as soon as we return.

Fortunately, the sketch pad is right where I left it.

I set to work. Jenna informs me that she's tired and wants to take a nap. I nod, and then she asks if I'd like to come nap with her. But I've been so focused on the new inspiration I've had for my project, I want to get to it. Plus I've never been much of a napper anyway. Come to think of it, neither is she. The ice skating must have worn her out. But as she's going off to our room, I hear her muttering to herself about how unromantic I am.

As I continue to sketch, I'm a little perturbed by that. I decide to ask my friends for ideas on how to do something romantic to surprise her. I make a point of avoiding Jordan, however. He always gives the worst advice.

"Hmm," Adam says, then digs out a folded piece of paper from his back pocket and skims it. "Oh, here's one I probably won't get the chance to use. Draw her a nice hot bubble bath and share it with her. I know you hate champagne, but maybe put some juice in wine glasses or something?"

Not a bad idea.

But now I need some female input on the best way to draw a bubble bath, so when Kat passes by my chair a few minutes later, I ask her if she's busy.

"Just taking my cup to the sink. What do you need?"

"Do you like bubble baths?"

She blinks. "Umm that's a random question. I don't get the chance to take them much, but yeah, they can be really nice."

She angles around as if to get a glimpse at what I'm sketching, but I close the book before she can.

"I'd like to make a bath for Jenna."

Kat's expression changes. "Oh, she'd like that. I can give you some ideas. Definitely get a couple bath bombs."

I envision an explosion in the middle of soapy water, like a miniature mushroom cloud rising into the air with violent force. Maybe like a geyser? That doesn't sound restful, relaxing *or* romantic.

She must have perceived my confusion because now she explains. "It's a product you put in the water and it dissolves, makes the water smell amazing and your skin silky soft.

"But why is it a… bomb?"

She cocks her head to the side and stares at the ceiling. "I actually have no idea whatsoever. You should ask Anna to pick you up some stuff to make her a nice bath. Make sure it's steamy but not too hot."

That's a good idea. Anything warm right now sounds amazing and I'm anxious to try it with her. The tub in our suite is definitely large enough to fit us both. Much more preferable than doing more activities outside where we can't even breathe without seeing every single exhalation as a puff of fog.

I pull out my phone and send a text to the concierge asking her to find some fancy bubble bath soap or bombs. And some rose petals.

# CHAPTER 15
## *KATYA*

"So… how's the prep for the big ski competition going? Are you getting your head in the game so you can show that man his place?" Mia asked me with a grin over a mug of afternoon tea.

I looked up at her from where I was studying the map of the Whistler-Blackcomb ski runs on my tablet and blew out a long, exasperated breath. This whole race thing had been taken way too far and people were taking this nonsense far too seriously, damn it all. It wasn't like—

"Don't disappoint me, now," she said with a sing-songy tone. "I've got fifty bucks for you in the pool." The what now? Oh hell, people *did* have money riding on this?

I arched a brow. "Your husband is a billionaire. With a B. And you're worried about fifty bucks?"

She dipped her head demurely and shrugged, a shy smile playing on her mouth. "It's my money, not his. Besides it's the principal of the thing. Girl power and all that. You need to show Lucas who's the boss."

"Just like you did with Adam?"

She snorted that adorable laugh of hers. "Right. Of course. It's the natural order of things."

I sighed into my own cup. This damn ski competition was officially making me miserable during a holiday I was supposed to be enjoying. I mean, when I wasn't stressing about whether or not my ski skills were up to snuff, I was stressing about why my husband was acting so preoccupied and brushing me off whenever I wanted to talk to him.

We were supposed to be up here enjoying the slopes, each other, and our circle of friends, weren't we?

I couldn't stop thinking about Lucas's mention of the black diamond ski runs when we left the helicopter. As I sat sipping my tea and wondering where the hell he'd vanished to, I pondered that. I've never actually skied on a black diamond run.

The truth was I'd been mediocre at best. I'd go up to the mountains with friends on weekends—usually Grouse Mountain or Cypress, which were much cheaper and closer to the city but not nearly as sophisticated and chic as Whistler.

Whistler was land of the double black diamond sure-death runs. And I'd be racing my husband on one of them. WTF had I been thinking, again?

I hadn't been thinking. That was the problem. I'd let a silly joke go too far, and then my ego and pride took over.

And it was almost certain that I'd lose to my husband, the man who'd skied all over the world. Now I had to come up with a plan to save both my pretty little neck *and* my pride.

That meant no black diamond runs. There was no way I could feasibly do it and survive. Compromise was in order, and since Colonel Sanders himself had brought up doing a blue slope instead of a black one, I could pin the change on him. Whoever smelt it, dealt it, and all that.

It *had* been his idea. I'd just be magnanimous as to allow him that gimme. I was generous like that. And he'd be ever so grateful, which he could express by providing me with numerous and mind-blowing orgasms.

My husband was very talented with his tongue. Lucky me. But since oral wasn't something to be enjoyed while encased in a full body cast, this whole black diamond scheme had to change and fast.

"Lucas suggested to me that it might be better for everyone to be able to watch us if we race on a blue slope instead of a black one. The black diamonds are much higher and don't really have many spectator opportunities."

That might have been a complete lie. It probably was, since the friggin' Winter Olympic alpine ski competitions had been staged here. But as long as nobody called me out on it, and so far, Mia wasn't, then I'd just let that sit.

She pushed her brows together and nodded. "Well, that seems logical. As long as it doesn't seem like a bore and too easy for either of you… why not?"

I sighed and inspected my nails—short and chipped as they were—and then gave a shrug. "Oh, it won't be boring. It's so beautiful out on the slope that I might as well enjoy the scenery while handing my husband his ass, right?"

She snorted again, this time louder.

So, just like that, I'd got us down to racing on an intermediate run. Thank God. Had I not nipped this in the bud, who knew where it might have progressed by the end of the week? Knowing Jordan, he might have gotten this ratcheted up to some crazy off-piste helicopter extreme skiing off vertical cliffs.

Thank goodness, I'd been badass enough to take control of this stupid-ass thing and make it my own. So no Raptor's Ride, Racer Alley or Catskinner for us. The alternatives sounded so much nicer—Crystal Glide, Cruiser, Crabapple.

Next, I had to face the hard reality that I needed refresher lessons as soon as possible. While my husband was obsessing over whatever the work situation was while trying to hide from me that he was stressing, I'd use his preoccupation to my advantage.

I'd secretly and discreetly schedule lessons with a private ski instructor.

"So are you in on my complex betting pool?" Jordan had the nerve to approach me a short while later, phone and stylus in hand as if waiting with bated breath to add me to his list.

I folded my arms across my chest. "Depends. What odds are you giving me?"

He squinted at his screen. "I haven't seen you in action, so no odds yet. I'm going out with your hubby later, so..." He shrugged and shot me a wicked grin.

*Butthead.* Sometimes I could just smack his face, but April would probably never forgive me for marring her pretty beast, so I'd better not.

"Are you in? And all bets are in real money, by the way."

I made a face at him. "*Real* money? As opposed to what, Bitcoin?"

He shook his head with a wicked gleam in his eye that I should have recognized before he opened his fat mouth. "Real money as opposed to Canadian dollars. Never trust money that colorful."

I shot him the bird. Sometimes that was the best way to deal with Jordan. Short, to the point, and it didn't elicit any more response from his big blabbermouth.

Besides, I had to get on my next step in the plan of managing this upcoming slope humiliation.

Within a half hour, I'd connected with our handy dandy concierge, Anna. Thankfully, on the phone via text. Whenever she was around in person, she seemed totally and utterly preoccupied with Jordan. Clearly she was just drawn in by his looks and hadn't spent enough time around him to realize how utterly annoying he was.

*I can make a few calls and see what's available, but it will be difficult to find an instructor. At this time of year, there's a big demand, since they are also available to the general public.*

I frowned at the phone. What the hell kind of answer was that? Weren't concierges here to get us special service? Wasn't that what they were paid for?

Plus I needed this, dammit. I wasn't going to let some woman who openly flirted with obviously-committed billionaires ruin my plan. I clenched my jaw and channeled the most obnoxious *Real Housewives* caricature I could muster and tapped back furiously.

*Isn't this service supposed to be high-end access at a high-end resort? And aren't you a high-end concierge who specializes in high-end experiences here?*

I never did shit like this, and I kinda hated myself, even if it was someone currently stepping on my friend's toes. I was incensed on April's behalf. So why not lay the attitude on thick? It might be the only way to get results from a person like her, who probably only thought pleasing the primary guests—Adam and Mia—were her priority.

*Oh, yes, of course. There are some instructors who will have openings. What I was going to say is they might be at less than convenient times, like late afternoon or dinnertime in order to fit you in.*

I frowned at my phone screen. Late afternoon? Dinner time? Skiing at dusk? A little bit beyond my skillset but doable in a pinch. I guess I could improve my skills in a baptism by fire.

*Okay. Please set me up for something during any of those times. I'm just very eager to fit a few lessons in as soon as possible, starting tomorrow.*

About a half hour later, she got back to me with a time. Being bitchy to a bitch got results, apparently. The appointment was set for early morning, as it turned out, the very next day. With a long sigh, I figured I'd just grit my teeth and do it. Then I could practice what I'd picked up in the lesson on the slopes later in the day.

Since I had a small window this afternoon, I decided to get started immediately, in my own element. Our fancy retreat mansion came fully equipped with practically every console system known to gamer-kind—PlayStation, Xbox, Occulus,

Vive, Nintendo Switch, the works. With a state-of-the-art TV, sound system, and all the bells and whistles to complete the package.

I logged into my PlaysStation Network account and immediately downloaded Steep, the downhill skiing game.

I was good at it, too. Well, I was good at almost any video game you put into my hands after minimal time learning how to work it. So sure, it wasn't the same thing as actually skiing—not even close. But it would get me in the mood and help me hone my reflexes for tomorrow's effort at the real thing. Doing this now was better than just doing nothing.

"Oh my gosh," Mia snorted as she sank down beside me on the couch. "You aren't seriously practicing your race against your hubby on a game console, are you?"

I pasted on my best appalled face, like I couldn't even believe she'd just suggested that. My eyes widened to form a big O, my jaw dropped. If I'd had a hand free, I may have placed it, spread-fingered, in the middle of my chest at the preposterousness of her suggestion. My thumbs were busy maneuvering the R3 and L3 toggles on the controller instead.

"Jeez, Mia. I can't even believe you'd suggest that. I mean— Come on. You're a gamer girl. You understand that sometimes a girl's gotta blow off some steam. That's all this is. It has nothing to do with that BS race. How could you even suggest that?"

Mia looked startled as if she was truly shocked that she made me angry. *Good.* I'd thrown her off the scent by making her think she'd wronged me terribly. It worked every time. Especially with Mia.

She proceeded to fumble all over herself apologizing. "I was just joking around. I'm—I'm so sorry—"

"It's okay. It's okay. No harm done," I offered magnanimously. Time to change the subject and get the focus back on her. The minute I wiped out, I paused the game. "So how's Adam? Still acting weird? Maybe it's a genius thing. I hear that they have to pay for all that brainpower somehow."

She opened her mouth to answer, but the front door opened, and some of the guys were spilling in. They had been down in the open game room at our resort playing a game of billiards and getting some beers. But apparently, they were finished.

I didn't kill the game fast enough, unfortunately. Damn, the gamer's reflexes were already rusty. Of course, once the fools caught wind that I was playing Steep, they had to chime in with their dumbass comments.

The best one came from Adam when I decided to restart the game—since they'd already seen what I was playing—and redo the downhill run on a timer. Maybe the route looked suspiciously like the K12 run that Lane Myer had to race down on one ski in the movie *Better Off Dead.*

In his best imitation of Johnny the paper boy, Adam mimicked, "I want my two dollars. Two dollars! *Ahhhhhh.*"

I guess if anyone was going to make a joke involving a movie from the 80s, it would be Adam, Mr. 80s-obsessed himself.

I had to wonder who I was fooling by skiing in a video game. But it gave me just a teeny modicum of control over the situation. At least I'd gotten us downgraded from a suicidal black diamond to an intermediate run, so there was that.

I could see the headline now: *Local girl decides to one-up her husband, breaks neck on mountain, makes him a widower after just nine and a half months.* Read all about it.

Of course, that assumed that *I* would be the one breaking my neck. Maybe I was heading into a situation where I'd become a widow at the ripe old age of almost twenty-seven. *Damn it.* At one time in the past, maybe I wouldn't have minded putting my now-husband, then just my annoying co-worker, in grave danger, but not anymore! I needed him to see to my sexual needs at the very least. Plus he was good to have around for other reasons.

Okay, okay, so I loved the dude. But I'd never counted on us being pitted against each other.

How the heck had we gotten into this situation again?

# CHAPTER 16
## *LUCAS*

I WISH MY SISTER WAS HERE TO GIVE ME SOME POINTERS. Julia was quite the accomplished downhill skier and always had been. Growing up, I'd let that be her accomplishment and stuck to my own strengths instead. Get me into a skiff with an oar in my hands and I'd out-row anybody. But skiing? Not really my thing.

And racing my wife down a mountain? *Definitely* not my thing. The only place I wanted to race her was to the bed. While naked. The more bouncing from her, the better.

I looked down the mountain from where I stood at the top of the run and sighed. Even though the race was being downgraded to an intermediate blue run, Jordan had coaxed me on this more complex run as a way to get back into the game. We stood off to the side, having just descended the chairlift where I was psyching myself up to try this insanity. I could probably count on one or two hands the number of times I'd attempted a black diamond run before—and this was a double black diamond. Jordan and April beside me appeared ready and raring to go, and equally annoyed by my delay.

Jordan had been egging me all day to get off my ass and practice. Apparently he had money riding on this race and I was his prize horse.

Well better a prize horse than a jackass, which is what *he* currently was.

"Come on, man. We've been standing here for almost fifteen minutes already. Let's get going," Jordan huffed, slapping his shiny snowboard down onto the snow and hooking his foot into the bindings. April stood beside him, the picture of a perfect slope bunny. Teal jacket and ski pants, hot pink gloves and hat. Expensive goggles, skis, poles, and boots to match. She stood poised to push herself down the mountain at any moment. From the bits and pieces I put together over the years of socializing with them, I'd been given the impression that April had been raised with money, too, and was therefore probably not a stranger to the slopes. I was likely about to disappoint both of them with my own skills.

"Why are you betting on a horse that refuses to run?" April said to her boyfriend with a laugh in her voice. Then she gave me an apologetic, almost sympathetic smile.

I frowned. "I ain't no thoroughbred. And why are we on this advanced run when we've already agreed to an intermediate one?"

Jordan made a dismissive gesture with his hand. "Boooooring. Live a little, bro. So the race is going to be on one of the blue baby runs, but if you practice on this double black diamond, you'll be all the more prepared to kick her ass."

"I have zero interest in kicking my own wife's ass, thank you. She has an amazing ass. The last thing I'd want to do to that ass is kick it. "

Jordan leaned in, as if explaining himself to a child. "*But* you don't want to be stuck *kissing* that ass for the rest of your life either, am I right?"

"I wouldn't mind it if *you* kissed my ass a little more once in a while." April quipped to her boyfriend as she adjusted her scarf where it was tucked inside her jacket. "Are we going to get going anytime soon? We're burning daylight, here, and it's getting cold."

"Yeah, yeah, yeah, just give me a minute." I turned the end of my skis toward the top of the slope. There, fearless skiers and snowboarders were slipping effortlessly off their chairlift and moving straight onto the piste.

"Alright! Here goes nothin'." Jordan had finally lost his patience and pushed off to get momentum as he hit the lip and made his effortless way down the dizzyingly steep slope before us. April, with a sigh of delight, pushed herself forward with her poles and followed suit. With a sizable gulp, an adjustment of my goggles, a grip and regrip of my ski poles, I haltingly slid down after April.

I didn't make it far before trouble arose. Maybe I hit a patch of ice or a rock—who knows, it might have just been a puff of air that didn't agree with me. Down I went, sliding sideways on my thigh and ass until I hit a flat part and slowed to a stop.

Ouch. Snow looks much softer down in the valley or anywhere but a gazillion feet up on the side of a cliff. Luckily, I was well-practiced at getting up from a prone position on my skis, so I pushed up on my right pole, as I'd learned, and dug into the slope with the edge of my skies. It wasn't elegant by any means. I probably resembled a tortoise on its back trying to right itself.

Once Jordan and April noticed that I wasn't directly behind them anymore, they skidded to a stop and waited until I could catch up with them. I had a sinking feeling that this was going to be a pattern for the rest of my way down, and it was going to take a lot longer than either of my companions would like. I suggested they go on ahead and I'd catch up, but of course, Jordan was having none of it.

"Dude, are you really that rusty?"

*No, I'm faking* it, I wanted to bite out, glaring at him from behind my goggles, which I'm sure he missed. "*Rusty* is one word for it, I guess."

He shook his head.

Maybe if he hadn't insisted on a fucking double black diamond run to force my return to the slopes, I'd be doing better.

"Go on ahead," I repeated.

"We'll go on a bit and find a good stopping place to make sure you haven't broken your neck."

Wonderful thought, *fuckyouverymuch.*

The next section of the run went about the same. But after that, they told me to go first. This allowed them witness to my humiliation in real time. Halfway down this next segment of the trail, I hit whatever mystical puff of air I'd hit before, lost my balance, and ended up sliding down the mountain the rest of the way—this time on my other side. At least I'd end up having an equal distribution of bruises across my body after all was said and done. By the time I'd made it down to the bottom—hopefully in this century—I'd end up looking a lot more like a popsicle than I cared to.

"Are you alright?" April pulled up her goggles to peer at me. Her deep blue eyes squinted at me in the bright light off the brilliant sunlit slope.

Jordan made a careless waving motion with his hand. "He's okay. Come on bro, get up. Let's get this going. You're warmed up now. No more falls. No broken bones, right?"

"I'm *fine*," I all but growled at him. Mercifully, he held out a hand to pull me up. Two more segments of the trail proceeded similarly. The falls seemed to be happening at random spots with no rhyme or reason. Sometimes I'd only make it a few feet before falling. Other times, I'd make it nearly the entire way to the next stopping point in the trail.

None of this boded well for the big race. Had I not been in waterproof ski clothing, I'd have been soaked and icy from head to toe.

At one point, Jordan declared me hopeless. "I'm getting tired of stopping and you're not letting me enjoy my ride and these amazing slopes," he grumbled. "We don't have anything like this in California."

"Tahoe has a lot of great runs," April amended.

Jordan still had his gaze on me, his mouth working. "Maybe you should concede now and save your neck while it's still intact."

"Maybe you should just go about your day and leave me the fuck alone," I snarled back.

"Down boy," he said, holding his gloved hands up as if in surrender. "Easy there."

Getting up once more, I brushed off the snow as best I could and refortified myself, steadying on my poles.

"You could just try and talk her out of this. If she's not game, sweeten the deal by agreeing to be her willing sex slave for the whole of next year." Jordan shrugged. "But that option loses me money, so I'm not in favor of it."

"Thanks for the negotiation tips." I growled.

"That sounds like a great idea, Jordan," April nodded enthusiastically. "I think you and I should have a similar deal. Loser of a race to the bottom from here is committed in sexual servitude to the winner."

Jordan cocked his jaw at his girlfriend. "You only want to do that because you know that you'll win. I ain't no fool. I won't take that deal."

April struck a pose and stuck her lip out in an exaggerated pout. "Well you suck, then."

A wide grin crept across his face. "If you're lucky, yes, I *will* suck. Tonight."

"Can you two do your foreplay somewhere else, please?" I snapped waspishly. Some of us were standing here trying to figure out how to get through the next couple of days without breaking their neck on a mountain thousands of miles from home.

"Alright, bro. It's probably not going to be pretty." He pointed down the slope. "Go that way, really fast. If something gets in your way, turn."

I gave him a gesture to show him how much I appreciated his helpful advice. With a laugh, he turned and pushed off without giving April any warning. She yelled after him and then pushed out onto the slope, quickly overtaking him despite his daring and flashy snowboarding moves.

I sighed. As irritating as they were, they were sure making this look a lot easier than it really was. I squared my shoulders in preparation to follow them at my much slower pace. There was no way off this mountain but down this damn hill. After waiting a few moments for Jordan and April to clear out, I gritted my teeth, bore down on my poles, and pushed forward, praying wouldn't kill myself in the process.

A long time later—by the aching of my body, it felt like I'd aged years, at least—I made it to the bottom of the mountain. I was sore from the crown of my head down to my ankles and walking like an octogenarian.

This day had not been good to me, and I'd had to put up with more ribbing from Jordan even later that evening back at our cabin. If he wasn't my boss—and I wasn't feeling my age plus sixty years—I may have hauled off and punched him to shut him up.

The kicker to an awful day? When my hot wife came on to me at bedtime. I was so sore and miserable, even after taking maximum doses of Motrin, that I couldn't deliver what she was asking for. So, feeling like an eighty year-old man in more ways than one...

I almost, *almost* suggested calling off the race. But she brought up the race right after my failure to—ahem—launch. Since my ego was even more bruised than my body, I couldn't let it go.

I just needed more practice—on an intermediate ski run.

And more painkiller. Definitely more painkiller.

# CHAPTER 17
## MIA

FOR THE SECOND DAY IN A ROW, I POPPED OUT OF BED early, and Adam was still dead to the world. We were both early risers out of necessity these days, but I rarely was the first one out of bed. I tiptoed out of the room, letting him sleep. He was still acting weird, and we hadn't gotten much further than the skinny dipping/death by imaginary bear shenanigans in the hot springs down the lane.

Part of the group had opted to ski again today. Part wanted to participate in our scheduled activities. We enjoyed a lovely, scenic ride in the Peak 2 Peak gondola that took us across the valley between Whistler Mountain and Blackcomb Peak. It was an impressive ride, though poor William had sat that one out, having declared he didn't do heights.

We enjoyed a tasty lunch in a small ski resort cafe on the top of a mountain and a little bit of tubing down a gentle slope in our neighborhood. All the snow fun we could ever want but never get where we lived.

That night, the entire group met up again, and we shared a catered dinner at home. April seemed stressed and upset for some reason, but when I cornered her in the kitchen, she wasn't talking. Maybe it had something to do with her thesis?

I put an arm around her shoulder. "Well, you know you can come talk to me whenever you need, okay? For anything."

Once game night began, however, my husband was the one exhibiting the strange behavior.

Adam was acting... *off.*

He wanted to hold hands a lot—much more than usual. Like the entire time my hand wasn't otherwise engaged in something important like holding cards or rolling dice, it was held by Adam. No complaints here. What woman didn't like having a hot hunk at her beck and call? I liked holding hands with him. But he also touched me in ways that weren't as...natural. It was awkward, as if he were reminding himself to do it.

*Touch Mia's waist once, her back twice, her shoulder three times.* Like he was working his way down a checklist—or going through a programming subroutine.

Somebody suggested a game of twenty questions. Each player chose a card from a stack and, without looking at it, held it up to our foreheads so others could read our identities without us seeing. Each of the cards listed a famous personage: historical, contemporary or fictional. You had twenty yes or no questions to ask in order to gather clues to your identity. The person who took the fewest questions to guess their identity won. If there was a tie, there'd be a play-off. Three of us made it into the play-off. Jordan, Adam, and me.

Except those two jerks cheated and I lost, all because they misled me on the very first question. "Am I male or female?" And they said male without question. And it took me far too long to figure out I was R2-D2.

"Not fair," I narrowed my eyes at them. "R2-D2 is not male and you said he was."

"You just used 'he' to describe him so therefore he is male," Jordan said.

"Well, that's neither here nor there. Droids don't have a gender."

"C3PO is male," Adam countered.

"That's only because Anthony Daniels, who is a man, voices him. But R2 doesn't even have a voice. How can you say R2 is male?" I made sure not to fall into the pronoun trap that time.

"Well what are you going to call R2, then?"

"Why is it only a choice between male and female? If you'd told me neither, I would have been able to figure out much more quickly it was a droid."

"Let's not argue about it.," Adam said, holding out a hand.

"I'm gonna argue about it because you two cheated."

Jordan glanced between Adam and me and threw up his hands. "I'm not getting involved in a lovers' quarrel. Or a marital spat, or whatever this is."

Adam's hand was still held out and he wiggled his fingers, like he wanted me to take it. Without thinking, I did. "I'm sorry you're upset, but R2-D2 is unquestionably male. C3PO refers to him as 'he.'"

"Pronouns don't prove anything, and it's a product of its time. If Star Wars were made now, maybe 3PO would have used the pronoun *they.* Who on earth decides robots have a gender?"

"Droids." Adam corrected, squeezing my hand. I released his hand in irritation and pulled back. He didn't let go. When the others were distracted in the process of setting up the next game, I turned to him. "Why won't you let go of my hand?"

"Because we're arguing."

"We're disagreeing."

"Okay, well let's please not argue about whether we are disagreeing or arguing."

I rolled my eyes. "My brain hurts. Can I have my hand back?"

"Not 'til we've resolved this."

I frowned at him. "Um. What?"

"We should hold hands while we disagree. And make eye contact. It's good for leaving a conflict without having hard feelings afterward."

I squinted at him. "You're acting weird."

And he held my hand for another twenty minutes, when we were well through the next game, a tournament-style multi-board play-off of Settlers of Catan.

"Emilia is the ultimate gamer chick. She's gonna beat everyone." Adam said while we played off during the winners' round. As with before, it was me, Adam, and Jordan, with the addition of Kat this time. Kat had taken umbrage at Adam's declaration, throwing him some major side-eye.

When he hopped up and offered to take our dessert dishes into the kitchen, half the room turned to me and asked. "What's up with Adam, tonight? Is he okay?"

I could only shrug.

And of course Jordan had to insert his less-than-helpful acerbic observation. "I think he's in the middle of suffering from a brain aneurysm, to be honest."

# CHAPTER 18
## *ADAM*

T HE NEXT DAY, WE HAD A LAZY MORNING BEFORE preparing for our big group outing—without Jordan and April, who were dining on their own and would probably end up getting engaged tonight. If Jordan hadn't adamantly sworn me to secrecy, I would have warned Mia.

But surprises were good, and she'd be thrilled for her friend.

This afternoon, the rest of us would be riding through back trails on snow machines to the edge of a glacier, where we'd join up with several dogsled teams to continue the journey through the mountains and watch the sun set from the summit.

But until then, we had a couple hours this cozy morning to do nothing at all. More than enough time to tick off more boxes on my checklist and possibly even finish it off.

I was a little worried, however. Emilia was getting impatient and, quite frankly, my body was on the same page as her. But my own stubbornness refused to blow this chance. Because that damn quiz and its dire prediction of a three-year or less marriage was still weighing on me.

But no worry, I'd developed the road map to get us back on track again—in the form of the handy dandy, technology-free checklist.

After breakfast, we went back to our room. I grabbed some wood from the nearby stack and started a fire to warm us up. Emilia was tidying up the place, gathering the dirty laundry and making the bed, since we'd requested minimal maid service in order to preserve our privacy.

My mind raced with the possibilities of what to do next. To help me think, I opted to take a shower so I could think it through.

But that got me nowhere except a lot cleaner. I toweled off, determined to go dig up my list and have a skim. I wrapped a towel around my hips and opened the door to the bedroom to get my clothes.

The room was tidy, the air warm from the now healthy fire. And Emilia was there, waiting for me. Full makeup, hair beautifully styled and her body stretched out across the bed, head propped up on her bent arm.

Her nighties had been getting progressively racier each night. And right now, she was wearing the sexiest one yet... an elegant weaving of scraps of white lace, straps and huge swaths of her gleaming bare skin.

Well... *gulp*.

Instant boner under my towel. *Holy shit.* She was stunning, all laid out like a five-course meal, waiting for me. And every single part of my body was ravenous and ready to indulge.

"You chilly?" I asked after clearing my throat. My voice, even to my own ears, sounded tight, strained. But I couldn't help noticing those deliciously erect nipples perking up to say hi, hence the question.

My tongue was already tingling with the thought of tasting them, suckling, even nibbling.

She licked her lips. "I'll be just fine when you come over here and take off that towel."

"Are you telling me you like my body, so I'll hold it against you?" I quirked a smile at her.

"Let's just say I'll make it worth your while." She extended one of those long, delectable legs and bent her knee so that I got a better view of the fact that she had no panties on. Shit, I could just jump on her now without removing a scrap of her clothing and have my way with her, any way I liked.

In fact, that sounded incredible.

Things were already feeling tight, achy, and painful down below. And clearly, the state of things was visible beneath the towel because her eyes focused on the bulge. My entire being and thought process was also focusing on that bulge at this moment, damn it.

I swallowed and my heart raced in the pulse at my throat. Maybe it would be good to get this out of our system, now, so we could go back to the checklist and getting the necessary things done to up our relationship game.

Because those nipples, those nipples looked very much like they wanted my mouth around them, my tongue lapping them up until she moaned and gasped my name. Yes, that was exactly what they needed. And what *I* needed, too.

I headed to the bed without another thought about the checklist.

Emilia's eyes lit up the moment I adjusted the towel, and my eyes scoured every inch of that luscious, rich skin—and there was a lot of it. *Damn*, this was a delicate, frilly, and trashy thing she was wearing, and I was here for it. All of it.

I wrapped my hand around her ankle and tugged hard enough to pull her down the bed toward me. "Come here. You are giving me very naughty thoughts right now."

She grinned wickedly. "Am I being a temptress?"

She knew exactly what she was doing, damn it. Temptress and all. Who'd have thought this sex goddess spread out on my bed was once the sweet and innocent—and easily riled—virgin I'd first met face-to-face in an impersonal and cold hotel conference room?  My eyes roamed the length of her. That girl was a million miles away from the woman she was now. Not that I wasn't irrevocably in love with both of them.

And I couldn't afford to let things slide. We were on a good track, and so far, the checklist had served me well.

Wherever it was. Where was it, anyway? Had it been thrown away? Damn it. I was reluctant to ask for my phone back because I really had wanted to prove to her that I could—and that I respected and honored her wishes enough to do it without a second thought.

But maybe I could get Jordan to grab the phone for me? He could unlock it and send the checklist to the printer in the business center. He'd give me incessant shit for it, but he'd do it.

Emilia was massaging me through the towel with her foot. Right where it felt the best. A blast of desire crackled through me in an instant. I dropped the towel and fell on the bed, pinning her beneath me. "Oh, I think someone is about to get fucked very hard and very well."

She writhed happily beneath me. "Yes to both."

I grabbed her chin roughly and pulled her mouth to mine, smothering hers in a needy and insistent kiss. She tasted like wine and chocolate and heat. I pushed my tongue into her mouth, hungry, greedy for more—for it all.

Didn't I used to have a photographic memory? I swear to God…why couldn't I see the list in my mind, like I usually could? Especially something I'd written down myself.

Emilia moaned, her fingers threading through my hair, sending hot shocks of pleasure raining down my spine straight down to my cock. The list had to be in the back pocket of my jeans. The jeans…where were they? On the bathroom floor? In the travel laundry bag? Shit, what if she'd picked up the paper and threw it in the fireplace while I was showering?

Emilia's breath panted between her lips as I shifted my hips to rest finally between her warm, open thighs. Exquisite. But, goddamn it, all I could think about was that fucking list and how I was probably violating the tenets of it six ways to Sunday. The advice had clearly said not to rely on sex to patch over problems in a marriage.

Wasn't I doing it right now? Would having sex undo all the good we'd been building the past few days?

I needed that list, goddamn it.

I gave in to the endless repeating loop in my head, pulling away from her. I moved to the nightstand. She stretched across the sheets like a cat, a lazy smile on her lips. Likely she assumed I was fetching a condom.

"I already grabbed one. Right here." She twisted at the waist to hold up the crinkly wrapper between thumb and forefinger. "See? Get back here. I need your cock—and you."

"Good, because we're a package deal." My eyes scanned her nightstand after having searched my own. No list there.

"I'll, uh, be right back, gotta hit the bathroom."

Her arm lowered slowly, face clouding. The laundry bag was in the bathroom, right?

It wasn't. So after running the sink for a minute and searching the back pocket of my jeans on the floor, I left the bathroom and slipped into our large closet.

"Adam?" she called from the bed.

"Give me just a minute. Be right there."

But no, it was more than a minute as I pulled from the laundry bag every article of clothing I'd worn since we'd arrived. I checked every single goddamn pocket, then went back and turned them all inside out. No fucking list.

Goddamn it.

By the time I'd returned to the room, I found it empty, the sexy lingerie in a puddle on the bed. Well shit.

# CHAPTER 19
## JORDAN

THE BIG NIGHT WAS HERE, AND I'D CRAMMED THE planning into every spare minute I'd had, finding ways to sneak off and communicate with Anna about every detail so that we were on the same page. The concierge was actually quite good at covering details I hadn't considered and used her connections to pull strings all over the resort.

I'd even had time to break away and go test the gondolas the day before. Anna had ridden with me and taken notes as we talked our way through how everything would go down.

Hopefully without a single hitch.

This was going to be the epic proposal. The one she'd be talking about for years to come.

No other Whistler proposal would be more romantic. I'd see to it.

So it was now only a matter of getting her there on time. I checked my watch again. April was taking a queen's age in the bathroom to get ready for this special night out together.

I hadn't even given her the details about dinner in the gondola, yet. No, that was all part of my epic surprise. I couldn't imagine having butterflies in my stomach. Butterflies were way too dainty for what I was feeling. No, these were definitely dinosaurs stomping around down there in the Land Before Time where everything was economy-sized, even the bugs. My entire gut was a forgotten prehistoric biome at war with itself.

And I was pacing so hard that I threatened to wear a path down to the very foundation of the plush carpeting in our bedroom.

"April, what's going on? Are you plucking the hairs on your leg one at a time?"

"I'll be out in a minute!" she called through the door.

"You said that ten minutes ago. We need to get going. Anna has set it all up and she's waiting to—"

Suddenly the door snapped open and she looked at me with burning eyes. "What? What did you say?" she snapped at me.

"I said we're running late. And Anna—"

"Why is she there? Why is *she* going on our date?"

I blinked. "Uh, because she's our concierge and I asked her to help arrange something special to—"

"Fine!" she stomped barefoot over to the closet bent and scooped up a pair of shiny black heels. She looked amazing tonight, in a deep purple dress that hugged her delicious figure and accentuated her curves. The tiniest of sparkles shot out when she moved, and the dress hugged her thighs in a way that made me want to hike that skirt up and push her against the wall.

She'd been off last night, when she'd gone to bed. Maybe too much to drink, because she'd had a horrible headache.

The kicker? She hadn't even wanted to spoon which was, secretly, my favorite part.

April was quiet when we got to the gondola lift. Her cute brows crinkled together. "I thought we were going to dinner. Why are we at the lifts? I didn't realize I'd need my snow suit."

"You don't. You're good."

She frowned, eyeing the pathway to the gondola roundhouse. "But then how am I getting over there through the snow in these heels? There's no way in hell these Loubs are getting wet."

"Here." I moved in front of her and bent so she could hook her arms around my neck. "Get up on my back and I'll carry you piggyback."

She didn't move for a moment, stomped her heeled foot in disgust. "I can't ride piggyback, you moron. This dress is too tight. I can barely move my legs to even take a long stride."

I turned around and eyed her. Wow, she was in a really foul mood. She'd never called me a moron before.

Without a word, I scooped her up and hoisted her in my arms. She let out a small shriek, but then I saw it... the first smile of the night! It was fleeting and shaky, but it was there.

Soon, we were in a gondola that had been set up with a table, long white tablecloth, fine china, gleaming silver dinnerware, and crystal goblets.

Our first course would be a charcuterie plate and champagne. April's eyes bugged out when got a glimpse of the spread. *Perfect.* Exactly the reaction I wanted. This would be epic. The proposal to end all proposals.

I'd get years of sex in the position of my choices for this. I'd get tons of leeway on the husbandly chores, too. I'd win all the husband points for being so incredibly original with the proposal, even if the mere thought of what it all meant still scared the shit out of me.

But we weren't ten minutes into the ride before I'd realized that not only had this been a bad idea, it had morphed into an absolutely terrible idea.

April wasn't afraid of heights. She had ridden the chair lift with no problems yesterday. But soon, she was sweating and shaking and suffering a full-blown panic attack.

When Anna got into the gondola at the other station to bring us the second course, April pushed past her and puked all over the pavement outside.

Anna looked at me. I stared at her. She shrugged.

And poor April continued to empty the entire appetizer course onto the sidewalk while onlookers cringed or turned away.

Well dammit, this was definitely going to be a night firmly etched in her memory, though not for the reasons I'd hoped.

So much for the uber epic romantic gondola ride, dammit. Back to square one.

# CHAPTER 20
## *APRIL*

L AST NIGHT HAD BEEN AN UTTER FIASCO. I KNEW I'D sorely disappointed Jordan by ruining his elaborate plans. Getting so sick on that gondola ride was as shocking to me as it had been to him. But, considering that I'd gone into that evening over-stressed, and weak from having undereaten the entire day, it shouldn't have been. Somewhere along the line, the anxiety and low blood sugar had combined and congealed into a full-blown panic attack that left me on my knees, blowing chunks everywhere. Dammit. I'd even got some on my new dress and in my hair. Jordan had stood beside that flirty little man-stealing wench and done nothing. Was it some kind of sign? That he didn't even help me hold my hair back when I puked?

Here I was the next morning, gingerly sipping weak, lukewarm tea at the breakfast table and contemplating whether or not my stomach was still too tender for food.

But I really didn't want to be around people or talk about the things that had stirred up my gut. So I opted out of the afternoon activities without really even understanding what they were. Some nature hike or whatever. I was opting out of peopling for the day.

I'd rather curl into a ball in the middle of my bed with my e-reader and the trashiest book I could find. The trashier the better.

Or maybe a comfort read. A treasured reread was always a sure bet. Even as I wallowed in my current misery, my inner book-nerd self rejoiced. I hadn't had time for a me-read in months.

When I heard that Jordan was following suit and also opting out of doing the people stuff, however, my plans changed. Because that meant we would have the mansion to ourselves.

And maybe I could repair a little of the damage my weak stomach and anxiety had caused the night before. Anything to keep him from getting drawn away by Miss Pretty Blonde and Petite.

It was time to have an open conversation about what was going on—no champagne, no fancy dates.

I'd wear my sexiest lingerie. We'd do a little heavy petting, and then I'd talk to him, *really* talk to him, and ask him directly what was going on. *And* I'd ask him point-blank if I should be worried about Anna the snow bunny.

The good news was that he was very attentive to me all morning, making sure I had something to settle my stomach, asking me how I was feeling. A very sweet Beast.

After he assured me he was staying in, I took a nap, had a relaxing shower, and indulged in a little self-pampering.

Then I went looking for my brand-new piece of sexy lingerie. I'd ordered it special for this trip as a little post-Christmas present for the Beast. But it wasn't anywhere obvious, and I found myself digging through every drawer containing my clothes. The concierge or her assistant had unpacked for me.

What the hell had she done with it? Had that little snow bunny sabotaged me?

With increasing frustration, I made a second pass. This piece was stunning, and expensive as fuck, and I wanted it wear it this afternoon!

I moved to the closet—not there. Double checked the suitcase I'd brought it in. Nope.

With a gasp of annoyance, I proceeded, still naked and wrapped in only a towel, to search *his* drawers for the damn bag. Nothing was obviously there, but to be sure, I reached my hand in and sifted, feeling for the bag or the tags or something. I was desperate, damn it! Once I hit his sock and underwear drawer, I was sifting two-handed and frantic to find the damn thing. I didn't.

Had she really sunk so low as to hide my lingerie? What was next? Frame me for murder and have me hauled away to some Canadian prison in the arctic? My heart raced and I only grew more frantic in my search.

When my hand brushed against a hard lump in a bundle of his socks, I froze.

I glanced over my shoulder at the door. It was still closed. I pulled the ball of socks apart to see what it was he'd stashed in there. Maybe it was a burner phone he used to communicate with Anna? I heard dudes did that when they were cheating. Hell, who knew, maybe it was a bottle of Viagra, so he could keep up with me and the demands of someone else?

My heart raced and my stomach roiled, threatening to bring up the small bit of food I'd eaten earlier. *Not again.* Please not again. I'd done enough puking for a year last night....

The small aqua blue box sitting in my hand was definitely not a phone. Nor a pill bottle.

Gulp.

The packaging was instantly recognizable due to the trademark Tiffany blue color. Was this for me? With another guilty glance at the door, I popped the lid on this puppy to get a gander at what was inside.

The box lit up with a flash to showcase a huge ring—white gold with a gigantic egg-shaped diamond resting atop it. Two-point-five, maybe three, I guessed. Extra clear, pure color—I'd bet a D color grade. This thing had most definitely cost a rock star's ransom.

I blinked. Stared. Blinked again.

What the hell was this? An engagement ring? In Jordan's drawer? *My* Jordan? Jordan Guy Fawkes had an engagement ring stashed among his personal effects?

Was this the apocalypse? Cats and dogs living together, mass hysteria?

What... what... This did not compute.

I tried to suck in a breath but found I couldn't. Stars were forming at the edge of my vision. I was maybe about one gasp away from hyperventilation.

At that moment, Jordan open the door and entered the bedroom. In my shock, I didn't think to tuck the thing away.

When he saw what I was holding, he froze in his tracks, eyes fixed on the box beaming bright on the shimmery rock inside.

He looked a lot like a man who'd just had his junk flattened by a steamroller.

He seemed to recover quickly, his stance loosening. With one hand he rubbed at his jaw. "Uh, oh. I see you found William's ring."

I blinked, stared down at the box, then up at him again. "Huh?"

He took another step toward me, eyes narrowing when he saw I was still just wrapped in a towel. "Yeah, William asked me to hold on to it for him. He's planning to ask Jenna while we're up here." He held out my hand for the box.

Now I was the one frozen and uncomprehending. So many possibilities and scenarios had just raced through my mind that they played on super-speed like some kind of weird movie montage. Slowly, jerkily, I snapped the box closed and handed it to him.

Then I blinked again. It made sense, after all. Much more sense than Jordan himself owning and engagement ring.

I bit my lip guiltily. "I was... I wasn't snooping, I promise. I was looking for my... well looking for something that I bought, but it's nowhere to be found. So I peeked into your drawers to see if maybe it had been shoved there. I don't like that the concierge unpacked for us, and I can't find my things!"

Good. Shade thrown on the concierge-bunny in the process. Excellent.

He stared at me, tilting his head. "Are you, are you feeling okay, babe?"

My eyes were still fixated on the box. When he noticed, he shoved it into his pocket.

I swallowed, then pushed up from my kneeling position on the floor to sit on the bed, suddenly chilly in the damp towel. "I'll be fine. I'm just annoyed because I wanted to wear something special... for you. Since we'd be alone this afternoon."

His brows twitched with interest, but at that moment, I shivered. "Let me get a fire started in here, and I'll get catering to bring in some munchies. And we'll have some nice alone time. Maybe get up to something fun and dirty. How does that sound?"

I frowned, still thinking about that ring and about poor William going to all the trouble of shopping for it—probably taking somebody ill-suited to the task for advice, like his cousin Adam or someone. Poor guy. Then stressing over hiding it so she wouldn't find it and having to plan something elaborate, just to ask a question and give her a piece of jewelry that might not even be to her tastes. God, I hoped it wasn't to her tastes.

I mean the diamond was big but...

Jordan was staring at me perplexed now, expecting an answer. "Sorry, I'm just feeling bad for William."

He blinked. "What? Why?"

"Someone needs to tell him not to propose to Jenna with that ring. I mean, just between you and me, it's fucking hideous."

# CHAPTER 21
## JENNA

I WAS SHIVERING, DAMP WITH SWEAT FROM OUR HIKE, AND dying for a steaming hot shower. Instead, I sat huddled in front of the fire in the living room, because William had blocked me from entering our suite.

He had a special surprise for me, he said and asked me to wait. And he'd been so sweet about it, how could I possibly complain? No, I could only sit here and wonder what he was up to in there.

I hoped it wasn't something like him getting suddenly shy about dressing in front of me. He never had been but... life with William meant there was seldom a dull moment. I loved it all.

But did he love it as much as I did? Maybe dealing with my neurotypicalness day in and day out was wearing on him?

For that matter, did he even still love me? And how could I get him to tell me those three magic words without prompting him to say it out of obligation? Or because I asked him to? And on that thought, why was it so important to me that he say the words without prompting and to say them often?

Whenever I said them to him, he usually didn't reply in kind.

My thoughts were interrupted when I realized William was standing beside me.

"I'm ready for you to come in, now."

About time! I was really feeling cold, even standing by the fire.

"Aren't you cold?" I asked him, finding it hard to believe that he wasn't, especially after all that complaining during the ice skating.

"I'll feel better soon. Hopefully you, too."

He escorted me back to the room and paused at our doorway, allowing me to enter first.

"I just want to get out of these clothes and warm up in the shower." I sent him a playful look as he entered and shut the door. With a sigh I yanked off my sweater and shirt. "Wanna join me?"

He shook his head. "No. I won't join you in the shower."

My spirits sank a little. It was difficult getting William to try new things, but we had showered together before. He hadn't said anything about putting that on the *never again* list. In fact, I'd thought he rather liked it.

I pulled off the rest of my clothes and hurried to the bathroom, suddenly overtaken with the urge to shiver. But I stopped short of going to the shower at the far end of the bathroom, because the large sunken bathtub was full to overflowing with a mountain of sparkling bubbles.

Oh my gosh! It had been ages since I'd enjoyed a bubble bath! How wonderful.

"You did this?" I asked him, my jaw dropping and my eyes wide. Without waiting for his answer, I stepped over the polished bamboo lip, across the natural stone tile and into the granite tub. Sliding my entire body into the cocoon of fizzy bubbles, I sighed deeply. The temperature was perfect, and my skin tingled, swaddled in warmth. "Oh my god this is amazing."

There were bunches of roses in glass vases set all along the back edge and the small fireplace here had been lit, too, to add to the warmth. And candles! He knew how much I loved my candles. I was always burning a votive or three at home. Sometimes he complained about it being a fire hazard but never protested beyond that.

My William.

He smiled. "Adam gave me the idea when I asked. And the concierge provided the necessary products. And then I used a thermometer to—"

I laughed. "Take off your clothes and get in here."

He nodded soberly. "I was going to ask first if you minded—"

"If I *minded*? Since the moment I saw this amazing bathtub in here I've been wanting to take a bath with you."

He needed no further assurance than that. William began to remove his clothes and carefully fold them, painfully slowly.

"Just throw it in a big pile for now. It all has to be washed. Get in here! Your lady has given you her sincerest wish." I wasn't above pulling rank when I needed to. William responded well to the language and code of chivalry, even when we weren't participating in meetings at our medieval reenactment society.

As I'd anticipated, it worked, and he was soon sliding into the water opposite me. We smiled at each other across the bubbles. "I was cranky that you were making me wait in my damp clothes but now I'm happy. It was worth it."

He smiled. "Good. I was hoping. And it's dark right now, or there'd be a beautiful view of the mountains right here. I drew the curtains instead because it would be very easy to see inside. Nobody gets to see you naked besides me." He gave me a very solemn nod. "Oh, and probably your doctor, but I try not to think of that."

I laughed again, leaning back and sighing in pleasure.

"The concierge suggested I pull the roses apart to float them in the water but I didn't have the heart to tear up perfect buds."

"I agree." I basked in the heat. "Wow the tub is even heated, too. How ingenious. So the water will stay warm."

William frowned for a minute. "It does have that feature, yes. But until you just mentioned it I had forgotten about it. Would you like me to turn it on?"

I sat up, definitely feeling the heat, my skin flushing. In fact it was starting to feel a little *too* warm. "What do you mean? The water is definitely feeling warmer the longer I sit in it."

William blinked and tilted his head toward the lip of the tub where the temperature controls were. "It's definitely not on."

Suddenly my skin wasn't just warm, it was on fire. Like burning. And not in the way that I'd feel as if the temperature had been turned up, either. With a sudden sinking in my stomach, I looked up at him. "Wil, what did you use for the bubble bath?"

William brightened, tearing his eyes away from the heating controls. "Oh, Anna, the concierge, was very kind to provide me with a very fancy bubble bath in a champagne bottle." He held it up. "See? Even has a French name that I could never ever pronounce."

I blinked, my vision slightly blurry. Maybe it was the steam but I was feeling decidedly unwell. My eyes were tearing up. "Shit, please don't tell me there's jojoba oil in that."

I lifted my arm out of the water and took one look at it. I was redder than a sunburnt lobster. The skin so shiny and brilliant it almost glowed. "Fuck."

William was scouring the ingredients label but I was in no mind to wait for that. I jumped out of the tub and shuffled as best I could while trying not to slip across the slick stone floor. I needed the shower and I needed it *now*.

I frantically scrubbed every inch of my body with soap—which made it sting—when William approached, his entire body tense with anxiety. "It definitely has jojoba oil in it. Why did I not know that you are allergic to that?"

"Because I never had a reason to tell you. You've never purchased any of my cosmetics or bath products. And I check everything meticulously."

"You need something. Tell me what you need. I'll go to the store."

"I need some antihistamine. But there's a medicine cabinet..."

Before I could say more, William was at the medicine cabinet, tearing everything out of it and poring over the labels. Apparently, there wasn't anything there he could use because he then bolted from the room. He was buck naked, so I had no idea where he was expecting to go from there. I'd go after him, but my skin was a shit show right now. I'd been submerged up to my shoulders in that water, but fortunately, it had never touched my neck, eyes or face. There was some comfort in that, at least.

The rest of me was red, inflamed, and a rash was forming. I had turned the water temperature down to tepid. I moaned with every painful throb.

Suddenly someone called from the doorway into the bathroom.

"Jenna? Are you okay?" It was Mia.

Well it looked like William had called in the cavalry. "Just a minute!" I called. "I'm naked. Let me grab a towel."

After making sure the soap was all gone, I turned off the water and wrapped a towel around me—but couldn't pull it tight. Wherever the terry fabric touched my skin, it hurt. And I was beginning to get a headache. Even my hands felt swollen.

Mia took one look at me and her eyes bulged. She went into doctor mode immediately, reaching up to press her fingers to the sides of my neck. "Do you have any risk of anaphylaxis? How allergic to jojoba are you?"

"I've never had an anaphylactic reaction before. I just get redness, sometimes rashes."

Her hands were still on either side of my throat. "Swallow."

I did as she asked. Then she turned to flip on all the lights and examine my skin. "Your hands are swollen. We need to get you some antihistamine, stat."

"That's what I told William... did he run and fetch you?"

She glanced up at me, then she put her thumb to my eyelid to hold my eye open and asked me to look left and right. "He ran out of your room shouting."

"Was he—was he naked?"

Her brows crunched together, and she looked at me funny. "No, he was wearing sweatpants and a t-shirt, why?"

I shook my head and waved her off. "It doesn't matter. I'm worried about him."

She shook her head. "He was very worried, but when I heard you were having a reaction, I raced in here and didn't really pay much attention to what he was doing. You washed all the substance off? Are you feeling any lesions? I see a bit of rash forming."

"Yeah I washed it all off."

Mia lowered her hands and stood up from sitting beside me on the bed. "There's a first aid kit in the bar. The concierge pointed it out our first day here, and I inventoried the contents to make sure it was good. I remember seeing some antihistamine tablets in there. I'll go grab them and a bottle of water. You might want to find something loose-fitting to wear or just slide under the sheets. The meds are going to make you sleepy anyway."

"Please, can you find out if Wil is okay? I'm worried that he's going to blame himself for this. It's my fault. I didn't tell him I was allergic to jojoba."

Mia was almost out the door already. "I'll put Adam on it." She left the room at a run.

I chose to pull the towel off my body—it felt like prickly sandpaper by now, and just slide into the sheets naked, but not before performing a brief inspection of my skin. A small rash of little red bumps was starting to form, but there were no lesions. Thank goddess.

Nevertheless, everywhere my body touched the sheets was painful, and my joints ached like I was arthritic. With a loud groan, I settled back against the pillows, and by then, Mia was back by my side with a bottle of water and the pills. I swallowed them gratefully.

She opened another foil. "Take these, too. Painkillers. You're going to need them."

I did as she asked, and then looked up at her with pleading eyes. "William?"

Her mouth thinned. "Well, I couldn't find Adam, but Jordan told me that William was so frantic he practically ran barefoot out into the snow to buy your medicine. Adam jumped on it, got him to put on his shoes, and they went out together. I can't text Adam to tell him to come back because he doesn't have his phone. But we have everything you need right here. I'm not sure what shape William's in, but I'll make sure to sit him down and explain everything to him when they're back."

I blinked. "Okay."

"Feeling sleepy yet?"

I nodded lazily. "Yeah."

"Good. You're going to need to sleep this one off. I'll let everyone know you're out for the night's activities. And I'll make sure someone stays here to keep an eye on you."

I think I muttered a reply, but I can't remember. Sleep, blissfully, was overtaking me, and the burning of my skin was just a distant awareness now.

Sometime later, I stirred, aware that I was painfully thirsty. I said as much aloud to the room, as if there might be an entire audience waiting with bated breath to serve me at my beck and call. In truth, there was just one. A vigilant knight perched on the edge of the bed, holding my hand and watching me carefully. Before I could even finish the request, he held out a cold bottle, carefully tipping it toward my lips so I could swallow it with a minimum of effort.

"Thank you," I whispered, letting my head fall back against the pillow as he replaced the bottle on the nightstand. "What time is it? It must be late. Why don't you come to bed?"

"I need to make sure you're all right. Mia said you need more pills, every four hours, and it's almost time. Will you be awake for seventeen more minutes?"

I smiled. "I think it's okay if you give them to me now. But first..." I reached out and took his hand. "I want you to promise me you'll get up and tend to yourself, and for goodness sake, go to sleep. I'm not a baby. You don't need to fuss over me all night."

"I did this."

"You didn't. Stop it." I struggled to sit up but his large hands went to my shoulders, holding me down. "What do you need? I'll do it for you."

"You can't. I have to pee."

There was some hesitation, as if he were devising some way that he *could* do it for me, but I gently batted his hands away and got up. I felt ever so much better. The reaction had mostly passed, with only the most minute soreness in some of my joints, vestiges of the inflammation.

When I returned, William held out the pills and the glass again. "I guess you can take it nine minutes early."

I thanked him and took the pills and water. He asked if I was hungry, and I said no. "Have you eaten dinner?"

William shook his head. "They brought back some food for both of us from their dinner out but I haven't wanted to—"

I pointed to the door. "Go. Now. Eat. If you don't, I'll be upset, and I might break out in hives again." A total untruth, but I knew enough about my stubborn sweetie to know that he wouldn't leave my side while he thought I was ill. "Or better yet, put it on a tray and bring it back here. I'll lie next to you, and you can eat your dinner and be right beside me, okay?"

I was forever devising compromises for him. And they worked and made us both happy. It helped him feel more comfortable and more likely to give on things he might have stood his ground for, otherwise. These little tricks of the trade I'd devised to keep our relationship running smoothly—I suspected that he had devised many of his own, too.

Were we actually being grown-ups in a real and honest, fulfilling adult relationship? Why yes, yes, we were.

But I still couldn't fathom why it was so important for me to hear those words from him. I knew in my deepest heart of hearts how he felt. But I hadn't heard those words in over a year.

He returned to bed with a tray of food, immediately offering me some. I declined again and he started wolfing down his sandwich, obviously famished. And yet he'd only reluctantly left my side, and only because I'd insisted. If I hadn't woken up, he might have never had anything to eat for the night. Likely no sleep, either.

I could feel the pull of sleepiness from the new dose of medicine, my lids growing oh so heavy. As William finished his sandwich and leaned back against his pillow, I reached out and covered his large hand with my own. Here I was in a cocoon of warmth and security and guarded fiercely by my love. *I'm so lucky.*

"Promise me something, please?"

"What?"

"No, promise me before I tell you what you are promising."

"Um, what does that mean?"

"It means I'm making you trust me by promising to promise me something. Just do it and don't ask questions."

His head jerked toward me. "Promising to promise you—?"

"Wil, just do it."

"Um, okay. I promise. Now what am I promising?"

"Promise me you'll sleep tonight, right here, next to me. I'll be okay, but I don't want you to be exhausted. Tomorrow, I'll feel much better and want to do things with you, go out and enjoy nature and just be together. Promise me you'll go to sleep and not stand guard over me."

He sighed.

"You promised to promise me."

Even he laughed at that. "I suppose I did. Okay, I promise I'll sleep, and we'll go out and enjoy nature tomorrow."

"And each other. Enjoy each other."

He turned his hand upward to wrap around mine. "I always enjoy being with you. Except maybe when you are forcing me to promise to promise something and I'm confused what that even means."

My fingers curled around his big, callused hand. My mind was already drifting off to that warm fuzzy place. My lids drooped. "I love you, Wil."

He didn't respond. But his hand squeezed mine tighter. I have no idea when he stopped holding my hand, whether it was five minutes or longer. Knowing Wil, he probably sat like that for hours, reluctant to pull his hand away to even change his clothes for bed. Stubborn man.

Stubborn, sweet, adorable, and unique man. *My* man.

# CHAPTER 22
# WILLIAM

"So when do I get to see the project you've been working on?" Jenna asks me with that tone in her voice and the familiar glance—the one where she's trying to make it look like she's not forcing an issue, when she actually is. She peers at me out of the corner of her eyes without changing the position of her head.

"You've had opportunities to look at the book when I leave it unattended. Haven't you tried to look?"

Now she does turn her head to face me, her mouth open in shock.

We're trudging through the snow early in the morning, just after breakfast. No one else was even stirring besides Jordan, who's always up around sunrise anyway. He'd been sipping at his coffee quietly while reading financial reports on his phone.

I have to admit, I wasn't thrilled about the suggestion when it started snowing, but Jenna excitedly jumped up and down when she saw it.

"Fresh snow!" she'd exclaimed, and though I dreaded the thought of walking out in the cold again—and seeing the puffs of air escape my mouth with every breath—I humored her, dressed, and we went out. Now we were holding gloved hands and trudging through the fresh snow—another thing I didn't like.

Walking in snow was worse than walking in sand at the beach, only cold. And wet. At least I have the excuse to once again wear the scratchy, imperfect scarf that she made just for me with her own pretty, elegant hands.

Jenna stared at me, shocked by my suggestion that she would have peeked at my work. "I'd never look at your sketch pad without permission, Wil!" But there's something about the flush in her face, and it isn't just from the cold, that makes me think that she's at least entertained the idea. Regardless, I trust her implicitly. She's never lied to me, and I don't think a small issue such as this would be the reason she would start.

However, I don't want her to be curious about this. It's a surprise, after all. But something has been bothering her. She's been acting different since just after we got here. It's subtle, but for me, easy to detect.

She stopped beside an empty lot on the lane. "You know what we *must* do in fresh snow, right?"

I frown. "Go inside and sip hot chocolate?"

She snorted, the air escaping her nose like stream from a dragon's snout. She is beautiful, as always, but that image is not. I don't like seeing the breath coming out of her face, either.

"Snow angels! C'mon, Wil. There's the perfect spot, right beside that cluster of trees. Fresh and untouched."

"That's because people aren't meant to touch snow. The reason for gloves and scarves and jackets and..."

But she's got me by the hand, and she's tugging me toward the fresh mound of snow. Reluctantly, I allow her to pull me toward it. The moment we get there, she drops into the snow, laughing like a gleeful child, waving her arms and legs back and forth. "Make an angel with me."

With a long, drawn out sigh—every inch of which I see stirring around my face—I drop down beside her and imitate her movements. Admittedly, I have much less enthusiasm than she is showing. But it makes her happy, as she laughs some more, and I have to admit that I crave the sound of her laughter. I'll do anything to make her laugh some more—especially after the disaster that was yesterday. Today, I'm inclined to do whatever she wants whenever she wants it. I am her courtly servant in every way, not just as knight protector, after all.

But making a snow angel is making me absolutely miserable. First of all, I started out cold, and this makes me colder, even though I'm wearing my jacket and scarf. Snow has slipped down the back of my jeans. And second of all, I'm now wet, which makes the cold even worse. And wet clothes are utterly intolerable. As with yesterday and the fiasco of the bath, we'll be returning to the cabin in wet clothes. At least I know better than to start a bubble bath, that's for sure.

Jenna has completely bounced back from that horrid experience and there's no evidence whatsoever of a rash or even any type if illness. She's got more energy than ever. And while I love that about her, I hate that she's always wanting to be outside.

I love nature and the outdoors as much as she does. I've done many a camp-out with our reenactment group and have even slept under the stars a few times, but mostly I prefer my pavilion tent. Most of all, I prefer to be warm. I don't like cold. I don't like wet. She knows this. But I'll do anything to please her, so I'll do it for now.

It doesn't mean I have to enjoy it, though.

"Oh, you made an amazing angel!" she says, sitting up to examine my handiwork. "A very *large,* amazing angel. Here, let me help you up so you don't ruin it getting out of the snow."

She weighs only a little more than half what I do, but she leans back, gaining leverage, and helps me out of the snow. I'm now soaked down to my boxers, snow under my jacket and shirt. I'm extremely uncomfortable.

"Ahhh look, isn't it fantastic! Your snow angel."

"It's an imprint of my body in the snow, and it hardly resembles an angel."

"Use your imagination! It's great. C'mon, let's walk a little more."

I was afraid she'd suggest that. When do I get to suggest hot cocoa and a warm blanket—in dry clothes—by the fire? Maybe next time Mia decides to do a big friend retreat together, I'll suggest a tropical island. But that means sand, and I hate sand, probably as much as Anakin Skywalker.

I begin to think of other warm places that don't have sand that won't annoy me as much as being wet and cold does.

"Wil? Can I ask a question?"

"I've never prevented you from asking me questions."

She laughs. "Yes, I know. I was just saying that to, you know, get a new conversation started." We're holding hands now and making our way up the street toward the hot springs. If it didn't mean getting wet—and then getting back out into the frigid air— I might even consider swimming in anything hot. Maybe not soup, but—

"I wanted to ask you... please don't laugh. Do you love me?"

I frown, unsure I heard her question correctly. Then I look at her to make sure she's not making some kind of joke. Sometimes I'm slow picking up when people are joking.

But this must be a joke, because she knows damn well that I do. She's serious—no smile. It's not a joke. But how? She already knows the answer to that question.

I blink. "This is a ridiculous question, Jenna. And I fail to see the humor in it."

She shakes her head. "I'm not joking. I just... I need to... I want to know what you're feeling. Right now, right at this moment."

"Cold and wet, and now that you've asked me that, irritated."

"Irritated? By me?"

"Why ask a question to which you already know the answer?"

She frowns, her blond brows knitting together on her forehead under her fluffy pink cap. "I'm not saying I doubt you, Wil. That's not what I'm saying at all."

"That's good. Then there's nothing to talk about anymore."

Now that we are no longer walking and a slight breeze has kicked up, I'm beyond cold. Even the muscles on my neck are involuntarily contracting to join with the full body shiver that's happening. I hate being cold. And I hate being wet. And I hate unnecessary questions.

I'm irritated. *Pissed,* as Adam would say. Though I don't have any desire to pee my pants, though at least *that* would be warm. For a few minutes. Until it turned cold.

I turn and walk back towards the house. She can choose to follow me if she likes or she can let me walk back on my own. I'll make sure not to let her out of my eyesight. With relief, I hear her footsteps crunching in the snow behind me, but I don't wait for her to catch up. The cold is taking over all my thoughts right now, and they aren't pleasant ones. No one deserves to be around me when I'm this miserable.

"Wil, hold on a minute!"

I keep walking and I keep my mouth shut, desperate to get to warmth. By the time we're back on the doorstep, I wait just long enough to hold the door open for her but no longer. I can barely tolerate another second in this temperature and almost leap through the threshold to get inside. I'd bust down the door like a gorilla if I had to. Fortunately, the front door is unlocked, and that's unnecessary.

We take off our boots in silence, and I'm headed for our room, dying to jump into the shower but unwilling to do it before her.

With a sigh and a low, resigned tone to her voice, Jenna insists I shower first. "I have the fireplace, and I'm not as bothered by the cold as you are. Must be my Balkan blood."

I don't say anything beyond thank you and promptly warm up with a scalding shower and soft, warm clothes to change into. I'd rather be alone, but since I'm still feeling cold, I make us both hot chocolates in the kitchen.

However, as I sit by the fire waiting for her, she doesn't leave the bathroom until the hot chocolate can no longer be called that anymore. Now it's just room-temperature chocolate.

For fear of making anything worse, I leave the bedroom and grab my sketch pad from where I left it. Jenna eventually emerges from our room, but I'm so engrossed in my work that I barely pay attention to when or if she found the room-temperature chocolate I'd left for her.

# CHAPTER 23
## *KATYA*

I HAD AN EARLY-MORNING SKIING LESSON FOR THE SECOND day in a row after which, the instructor warned me not to do any of the resort's blue runs. "Just work on the green circle slopes this season and you'll be set. Green runs here are like blue, or even black, at some of those resorts in Southern California."

Here was one of my fellow countrymen taking the opportunity to exert Canadian superiority over my newly-adopted home. He had no clue I'd been born and raised in Vancity. I sure as heck didn't look like a California girl, though. I may work and live in SoCal but I was a Vancouverite down to the bone—bones that I hoped to keep intact throughout this current marital conundrum I found myself in.

Despite the instructor's warnings, I felt confident that I could at least make it down one of the intermediate runs in one piece. And today, I had the time to get some more practice.

I wasn't above noticing that Lucas was finding time to slip away, likely to get some practice on his own. But also to work, which was worrying. I didn't want to end up like Mia, who was constantly trying to manage Adam's workaholic tendencies by forcibly infusing balance—like renting an entire getaway villa for the two of them and all of their closest friends, for example.

Lucas had some online conferences with work colleagues, and he seemed to be really unhappy with whatever was going on at work. He most likely wouldn't take kindly to me expressing my sympathies, much as I would have liked to. Despite being married and deeply in love, neither of us had fully shed that competitive streak that ran through the baseline of our relationship. And for me to express sympathy might be interpreted as gloating.

And I didn't want to gloat. I just didn't know how to tell him I wasn't gloating.

So instead, I let him deal with his stuff and asked no questions and waited for him to volunteer any info he wanted to share.

Whatever Lucas had wandered off to this afternoon to do, I took advantage of the block of time to grab my ski equipment and head to the singles line on the lifts. I'd read a tip that the lift lines moved faster by opting to share a lift chair with a random stranger. And that would give me more time to get extra runs in before Lucas would even notice I was gone.

I could try one of the simpler advanced runs just to assess how I might do. I could always go down from there.

It seemed like a good plan.

But that plan didn't take into account how scary the advanced slope looked from the top of the chairlift, looking down. When I was supposed to slip effortlessly off the chair like all the rest of the ski bums and slope junkies, I balked.

When I got to the top of that black diamond run, I wouldn't budge. My butt remained firmly glued to the chair, riding it right back down to the hill again. If I'd gotten off at the top, the only way down was on the skis. And I definitely wasn't ready for that.

I made a complete loop—and sheepishly avoided the liftie's eyes as I slumped off the chair in shame. In reality, the idea of me doing a black diamond run was ludicrous—even for practice. I wanted my pretty little neck intact as long as possible, thankyouverymuch.

Once I'd taken that—*totally planned*—aerial survey of what a black diamond slope actually looked like, I was more than relieved that this stupid-ass race would be on a blue line instead.

Easy, right? Sure, sure, I could do this. I made my way to the appropriate lift for what appeared to be a much easier blue run and got into the singles line.

However, this time, instead of a woman on the other side of the chair, as had been the case on the previous ride, some dude fell in right next to me. A chatty dude—and from the looks of him, a park rat. He really liked to talk. About himself. And about how much he could shred, and rip up the slopes. I glanced around, seeing a bunch of other guys my age and older in the line-up. Most of them were eyeing the women. My particular yakkity yakker had zeroed in on me the moment I'd stepped in line. It's almost like they'd read some kind of shortcut from the same tired book on how to pick up women.

This dude-bro beside me was wasting no time.

And my wedding ring was buried under what felt like miles of leather glove, damn it. There was no easier way to scare off a dude on the prowl by flashing a little gold and diamond on the left hand.

"Hey there, I'm Robert. What's your name?"

"Persy," I said without batting an eye or even hesitating. It was a shortened version of my favorite gamer name, Persephone, so it wasn't exactly a *lie.* Why on earth would I give some rando my real name? I was married, for heaven's sake. *Very* married. Very happily married *and* sexually-satisfied, for that matter. I was only in this damn singles line because it was half as long as the other one. But for some reason, these dudes seem to think it was a fair hunting ground for hookups apres-ski.

I mean…talk about captive audience. Chat a girl up on the chairlift when the only way she could get away from you was to drop off the chairlift dozens or even hundreds of feet in the air. I threw him major side-eye while he boasted about his prowess on the slopes and how he was taking a rest on the blue slope.

With a sigh, I realized that, even during my single days, if I'd come up here to find a boyfriend, I would have just been stuck with one loser after the other. Well tick that box off on my list of *things I'll never regret not doing.*

"So, Persy, you come here often? Are you a big skier?"

"I guess you could say I come here every once in a while. I am from PoCo, after all. So it's close." Sometimes in touristy joints like this, a guy is hitting on a girl for a holiday hookup, so knowing they are a local really turns them off.

Well, apparently not so for Robert. He asked for my number before we were even halfway up. I told him we could work that out once we were off the lift. Then, when he slid off the chair to make his way over to the side, I proceeded to ride the right back down the hill once again.

No need to give poor Robert the wrong idea, right?

I actually ended up doing more riding on the chair than actually skiing down the mountain. If nothing else, it gave me a great overview of the resort.

With each ride, yet more guys, more obnoxious than the previous one, would try to pick me up. Finally I got the brilliant idea of pretending that I didn't speak any English, and instead mumbled some gibberish that might have passed for Norwegian or Swedish instead. I suppose I could have produced some broken French, but since we were in Canada, the odds of finding another French-speaker were too high for that stunt.

I mimed a few things and smiled and nodded and was spared still more cheesy pickup lines and bro boasting.

Okay, I skied down a few times, slowly and haltingly, and the instructor was probably spot on gauging me for a green circle slope instead of an intermediate one. But I was now confident that I wouldn't humiliate myself, even if Lucas did make me eat his powder.

He'd most likely win, and that was fine with me. Perhaps he'd be more likely to fulfill my sexual desires that night in order to celebrate his victory. He'd all but brushed me off last night, groaning like an old man with a hernia and refusing to change his clothes in my presence, for whatever reason. And he was as grumpy as a geezer, to boot. He could use the stress relief, too!

I was tired from all that chair-riding, so I hit the bar for a hot toddy with extra whiskey. And French fries to go with it, of course—with nary a cheese curd or drop of gravy in sight! I people-watched and reflected over the day's events, the missed rides, the deflected flirtations and crazy pickup lines.

Apparently, even though I could flash my wedding ring prominently here, it didn't make me immune from still more unwanted male attention.

Dudes didn't care. I got a couple drinks sent to me—which I turned down. A couple guys took the stool next to me—despite me setting my bag there as a deterrent. It got to the point where the minute a guy sat there, the first thing out of my mouth would be, "I'm happily married. Thanks, but no thanks."

These dudes seriously needed to up their game if they wanted quality companionship the likes of me, anyway. But it wasn't going to *be* me.

I already had my grump-for-life. And he was sexy and hot and everything these guys were not.

I'd just have to figure out a way to get him to put out tonight.

I cursed this damn race and my big mouth. If I'd been honest from the start, we would have been sitting in this bar together and laughing at the idjits as they tried to pick up the girls and got shot down, while drinking and flirting with each other.

I mean who really cared about beating him at skiing? I kicked his ass regularly at what counted—video games—and that was more than satisfying. Who cared if he was the better skier?

I heaved a big sigh and cursed my own stupid big mouth for getting me into this mess.

# CHAPTER 24
## *LUCAS*

Y WIFE WAS NOWHERE TO BE FOUND. THIS WAS A BIG mansion, but that's ridiculous. Her ski outfit and jacket weren't in the closet, either, so clearly she'd hit the slopes. What she wasn't doing was replying to text messages, damn it all.

We were here on the perfect ski holiday with close friends and had hardly spent any time together at all. Instead, I was stuck in this beautiful mansion without her, dealing with stupid employees who were out to make the other one look bad.

I was dealing with avoiding one friend—who was also one of the bosses. He kept referring to me as his *lame racehorse* who was going to lose him money. Like he'd miss one hundred bucks. He was a billionaire. I was about ready to cram a Benjamin down his throat myself, so he'd shut up.

I was avoiding the other boss because I didn't want him to get wind of my work struggles. Or the truth about my skiing prowess.

The only good thing going for me right now was that I'd found the perfect place in this mansion to avoid just about everyone—the third-floor library, with a full three-story picture window view of Blackcomb Peak.

My solitude only lasted about an hour—well physical solitude, anyway. Heath sauntered in and settled on a couch at the other side of the room. But as he had his earbuds in and phone in hand, he left me in peace, staying focused on his phone for almost an hour after that.

So once I was done, I drifted to the window and looked out over the gorgeous view. I pulled out my own phone and texted Kat to find out where she was. The afternoon was growing late, and I was bored silly sitting here on my own.

Heath started humming and nodding his head to something he was listening to. I cocked my head to glance at his phone and see he was on TikTok.

"This is amazing," he said almost to himself.

"What's that?" I asked.

"Sea shanty."

*A what?*

He pulled out his earbuds and hit play to demonstrate—a catchy maritime tune sung a capella that sounded almost like pirates singing in perfect harmony. He tapped his foot in time to the music, and I found myself nodding along as well.

"It's addictive." Heath grinned. "Kinda sounds a bit like some of the Irish songs Connor used to sing. That man has *such* a singing voice..."

I frowned, struck by the wistful tone in Heath's voice. I'd never met Connor, but Kat had informed me that he was Heath's former boyfriend who now lived in Ireland. Kat told me that he hadn't really been the same after their breakup last year.

I sank down on the couch beside Heath and he scrolled through TikTok and played a few more versions of the song, and before we knew it we were both singing about Wellermen and whaling along with the video.

"Addictive, right?" Heath mock elbowed me.

"Yeah." We glanced at each other and burst out laughing at the same time. It seemed so weird and random, really.

"You were sitting here listening to music from the nineteenth century. And here I thought you were sitting there playing Among Us and ruthlessly assassinating randos."

Heath laughed. "Well, that's also held a lot of appeal, too. Great way to vent frustrations. Maybe the sea shanties will overtake the Among Us addiction."

I shrugged. "Might be a healthier addiction. At least the sea shanties make you want to get off your ass and move instead of playing a game on your phone. Not that there's anything wrong with that."

"We're all hardcore gamers here, no one's going to think there's anything wrong with that." Heath grinned and then hit replay on the jaunty song, humming along to it, then letting his head fall back on the couch to look up at the ceiling.

"Damn, I still miss him."

"Well you know what they say about the best way to get over someone..."

Heath laughed and nodded. "Getting under someone else, yeah. Been there, done that probably a couple dozen times by now."

"Then what's another one? That concierge's assistant wasn't subtle about his interest in you..."

Heath shot me side-eye. "*So* not my type. Anyway, I think I'm done with the casual bullshit. I've never been good at it anyway."

I swallowed, trying to think of what to say. The mood in here had thickened, and I sensed that Heath really did want advice. I was no good at this shit—as most people who knew me knew. And until recently, with regards to romantic relationships at all, I'd been a very diehard and unbelieving cynic.

"Relationships are hard." It was all I could muster in my own lame way. It was true, after all. I was currently on marriage number two—and the one that was going to go the distance if anything was. But still, number two meant I'd gotten it wrong the first time—so *very* wrong.

Heath quirked a brow at me. "That's not something I'd expect to hear from someone who fell madly in love with the wife I fakely married him to last year. Should I be concerned?"

I laughed. I'd worry about being overheard, but no one was anywhere close to us and Heath had kept our secret faithfully. Kat and I might be a real married couple now—*and* truly in love— but it hadn't started out that way. And it hadn't been that way for at least the first six months of our marriage.

"No, I'm speaking generally. Nothing to worry about here, except maybe this crazy ski competition. I guess we didn't really say 'until death do us part' in our vows. Still, I sure as hell hope that means beyond tomorrow."

Heath grimaced. "If you're worried, maybe talk to her?"

I shrugged. "She seems to have her heart set on making me eat her powder."

He waggled his brows suggestively. "I think she'd be much happier if you ate something else. And it wouldn't be life-threatening."

I blew out a laugh. "You're absolutely right."

"Seriously, why don't you just tell her you're having second thoughts about the race?"

I blinked. I suppose I could. Why was I letting my ego get in the way of some frank marital honesty?

"For what it's worth, I've got fifty bucks on you, because I never ever heard her talk about skiing the entire time she was my roomie. Maybe she'd be relieved if you were the one to stand down first."

I thought about that for a while—since it was almost a couple hours before I did see her again. She had to tell me about how she'd gone up the black diamond lift a few times just to get the kinks out for tomorrow.

She seemed so enthusiastic about beating me, I didn't have the heart to back out now. Kat would have her win, and I'd get my own reward via a very enthusiastic and victorious wife in bed that night.

*Sigh.* Come white-out or wipeout, I guess we were doing this thing.

# CHAPTER 25
# *MIA*

FIVE DAYS INTO OUR WEEK-LONG TRIP, AND I WAS beginning to suspect that Adam, indeed, was suffering from an aneurysm. Or deeply stressed out about something. Maybe it was genuine withdrawal symptoms from his personal electronics? Should I offer him his phone back? Or should we start looking into 12-step programs for him?

*Hi, my name is Adam Drake and I'm a smartphone addict.* I could just picture it now.

With a sigh, I began straightening our room while Adam was on a snowshoeing hike with the other three guys. I had an appointment with the girls to sit in the infrared sauna in a few minutes.

Maybe I should honestly start worrying about him? What if he was having neurological problems? Or the onset of mental illness? I'd just finished the neurology rotation of med school a few months before. I remembered the signs—unusual and uneven pupil dilation. Adam's eyes were so dark it was difficult to tell, unless I was positioned very closely in a brightly-lit room. Tracking motion and answering basic questions were part of the screening. I made note to apply it next time I spoke to him.

I bent to grab the decorative throw-pillows that had been heaped on a nearby chair to replace on the bed. When I picked up the last pillow, a slip of paper fell to the ground. With a sigh, I grabbed it. He usually wasn't one for leaving trash around. Actually, for a man, he was pretty damn neat.

It was a list, written in his even, precise writing. Some of the items were checked off.

- *Lavish encouragement*
- *Hold hands even while you're disagreeing*
- *Find time in silence to gaze deeply into each other's eyes.*
- *Spend thirty minutes only kissing without touching each other or having it lead to sex.*
- *Spend time spooning and just talking, nothing else.*
- *For team work, find a fun project you can work on, together.*
- *Write each other a long letter listing all reasons, big and small, why you love each other*
- *Show spontaneity. Choose to do something wild and crazy together that you've never done before.*

My brow creased and... sudden understanding hit me.

No it wasn't a brain aneurysm after all. It was my husband glomming onto the fact that we'd made some low score on some stupid app quiz somewhere and him insisting we up that score, like a true gamer.

Min-maxing his real life. Oh, Adam.

Nowhere on this list did it say, *Ignore your wife in that sexy teddy sprawled out on the bed like a queen waiting for you to service her sexually.*

I contemplated how I might get back at him for this... a little spousal revenge never did any harm, right? I felt the inspiration for a practical joke coming on....

Except not, because he walked in on me while I was holding the list. He was back hours early—from the sound of it, all the guys were. "What—I thought you were going snow-shoeing today?"

He shook his head. "They aren't allowing it today because of avalanche risk.

I blinked. "Oh..."

"So we have the afternoon..." he said with a small waggle of his eyebrows. In one swift and very impressive move, he slid an arm around my waist and kicked closed the bedroom door. "What should we do with it?"

"Mmm," I frowned. "We could try to tick off more of the boxes on this list, if it weren't such a ridiculous a thing to do."

His frown mirrored mine until I held the list up and waved it in front of him. "I'm guessing your OCD hunt for this is what ruined what would have been some awesome sexcapades yesterday?"

Adam blinked and reached for the list with his free hand. I pulled it away from his grasp, because I'm petty like that. "I don't see 'Buy your wife a gazillion-dollar brand new gaming rig or piece of jewelry' on this list. Can I add that? Or maybe 'Give your wife no less than five orgasms every time you have sex.' I like that one even better."

He raised his eyebrows at me expectantly, wordlessly demanding I hand over his little programming flowchart for upping your relationship score.

"How about... you agree to become my willing sex slave for the next twenty-four hours?"

He narrowed his eyes, and his hand darted out, quick as a flash, and tore the list out of my hand. Then, with a wicked gleam in his eyes, he leaned in. "More like *you'll* be *my* willing sex slave."

I blew out a breath and rolled my eyes. "Promises, promises."

But he was glancing over the list again and tucked it into his back pocket. I should have tossed it into the fireplace when I'd had the chance!

He had his grabby hands all over me before I could even move on from the vision of that damn list reduced to a handful of ashes. And in a plot twist even I hadn't seen coming, I pushed him away. When he gave me that questioning stare, I pointed to the end of the bed.

"We need to talk."

His handsome features sobered. "That doesn't sound good."

"Come here..." I sat down and patted the spot beside me. "You need to toss that list."

After a brief hesitation, he took two strides and sunk down on the bed beside me. "I was just trying to do the right things. That quiz—"

"Was some stupid little bit of BS that someone wrote up for filler space on a pseudo-news site. They don't know us."

He blinked as he stared at me, then rubbed the back of his neck as he shifted. "Okay, but aren't you concerned?"

"By what? Do you think we have a bad marriage?"

He shook his head vigorously. "Of course not. But you have to admit, we are very busy people."

"We are. We don't see each other as much as we want to right now. But this is just a phase. A building phase. I have school, you have all the work. We're building a future right now. This is temporary."

"Temporary for at least a few more years."

I shrugged. "Sure, but in the meantime, we make the most of the time we do have together, right? I mean, you voluntarily surrendered your phone up here without the tiniest inkling of a fight. Because you wanted quality time with me. That's huge, and I really appreciate it." My hand darted out and I cupped his bicep, then let my hand slide down his arm slowly, relishing the firm muscle underneath his sleeve. I smiled. "I love that you were so worried about us that you made a list, even if the list was ridiculous."

His brows furrowed. "Ridiculous? What? You mean you didn't like staring into each other's eyes while we laid on the bed together?"

I bust out laughing. "That was weird, you gotta admit. When have we ever done that, and why would we? When I talk to you, I want to tell you everything and I want to listen to you talk about everything you want to tell me. And when we're not talking...."

"We should be fucking?"

I laughed. "I'm not gonna argue with that."

He lifted a hand, hooked it around my neck and pulled my head to him, tasting my lips slowly, firmly with measured movements. "I gotta admit I was driving myself crazy."

"Yeah, you tend to do that, don't you?"

He locked his other arm around me and pulled me down on the bed with him. I laughed and we faced each other. "I want to take this bikini off you with my teeth."

I laughed and pushed back on his shoulder so I could look into his face. "I don't want to see that list again... and for god's sake, stop with that bullshit encouragement. I mean, I love when you encourage me but let's keep it for more special occasions, okay?"

He kissed me again, pushing his tongue in my mouth. "All I can think about right now is how much I need to get inside you. I'm horny as fuck."

I smiled, reaching a hand down to cup his crotch. "Thank god for that."

There was a knock at the door. Jenna and Kat were yelling at me to get off my ass and meet them in the sauna.

Well shit, so much for hot afternoon sex. Adam lay back with a sigh, staring at the ceiling and ruffling his dark hair. I gave him a consolation kiss and whispered sweet dirty nothings in his ear to tide him over until we could get down to the real thing.

# CHAPTER 26
## JORDAN

*J*ESUS, *FAWKES, YOU FUCKIN' IDIOT! WHY DIDN'T YOU JUST TELL HER the truth?*

I ran a hand through my hair, curling my fingers to give it a tug, my mind on an infinite loop.

I'd been stunned to silence threatening a full-blown internal meltdown when I'd walked into that room this afternoon and saw her holding the ring box. So I'd done first natural thing that occurred to me. I'd lied my ass off.

Because all I could think was I couldn't just drop to a knee on the spot. Where in hell was the epicness in that? Imagine bragging to her girlfriends about her idiot fiancé who'd proposed to her while she was wearing nothing but a bath towel.

I'd lied to more than my share of women before, but never April. Well, until all this bullshit proposal business came about. What a complete and utter disaster—all of it. Right up to the fact that she hated the ring and had deemed it hideous. She never would have admitted that to me if I'd slipped it on her finger. She would have just loathed it in silence—if she'd agreed to wear it at all.

Note to self, find a new engagement ring stat, right after swiftly kicking Adam in the ass for his shit advice. Or maybe his shit advice had been revenge for the once or twice or maybe even three times that my advice had almost cost him his now-wife. *Whatever.*

I tore myself away from the view out the main dining room window and pulled out my phone to text Anna for more help. Ring-shopping at the nearest jewelry store was in order. And a new plan for how to pop the question to April.

Now what to do about damage control? Cover my tracks like a coward, or 'fess up and just take my lumps?

As if sent from the Universe, at that moment William entered from the kitchen with a steaming mug in his hands. I stared at him for a long moment, frozen in indecision.

The coward's way it was, then.

William's eyes flicked to me, and he paused to grab a few cold cuts and some fruit off the snack tray.

"Why are you staring at me?" He didn't look up as he filled his plate.

"I need to talk to you real quick… can we go to the kitchen?"

"I just left the kitchen."

"I need to… make sure I'm not overheard. Please?"

I saw, with relief, that it would take no further argument—which was actually pretty unusual for William. But after I pulled him aside and explained the situation, the difficulty began.

"I don't understand. Why am I lying to your girlfriend?"

My head ached from clenching my jaw. William. I loved the dude, but he drove me flat out crazy sometimes. "I told her I was holding the ring for you to give to Jenna."

"Yes, you said that. I'm not hard of hearing. I just can't figure out why you thought lying to your girlfriend was a good idea."

*Because I'm a dumbfuck.* I sighed and rubbed my forehead. "Just do me a solid this once, William? I need you to cover for me."

He shook his head. "*This once*? I do favors for you often, and it's too warm in here for blankets. Unless you needed covering outside? In which case—"

I held out a hand, my head throbbing. "Never mind, I'll think of something. But please, if she asks, can you just go along with it? Or change the subject without answering her?"

"It's not logical to keep such a big decision and a momentous question a secret. She should have time to—"

I cut him off, chopping with my hand. "Never mind your opinion of my approach, Mr. Spock. Just...will you do it, please?"

He paused, looked at me for a moment, as always without actually meeting my gaze, and curtly nodded. "I won't correct her if she approaches me with alternative facts. Of course, I'll have to tell—"

"Great! Please, just don't tell Jenna either, okay?" I slapped his shoulder and left him there, openmouthed and staring.

There was only a day left, and I had to find a ring and find it quick. I had an idea of going simpler by asking her tomorrow night when we rang in the new year. *With* a new ring, of course. I checked my phone. Anna had texted back and we were going to meet to discuss how she could help me find a non-hideous ring. I sighed. Hopefully Tiffany's offered refunds on $40,000 engagement rings.

I was in the middle of texting her back when April found me. "Jordan."

Uh oh. I knew that tone well. Without finishing the text, I hit send in a panic and shoved the phone in my pocket. I was sure it'd make absolutely no sense when Anna got it, but I'd finish the thought later. Now I turned to face my not-so-happy girlfriend standing beside the entrance to our suite.

She jerked her head toward our bedroom, and I held my breath, bolstering myself.

Once I was through the door and closed it after us, she spun on me, arms folded tightly. "We need to talk."

Without thinking, I checked my watch. I likely only had an hour or two before the shops closed, and tomorrow, New Year's Eve, might be iffy...

I glanced up at her and she stared at me, mouth open. "Did you actually just check your watch?"

Whoa. She wasn't just irritated. My girl was *pissed off.* "Uh, sorry. I didn't mean—"

Fuck, how to get the hell out of here and go get her a damn acceptable ring she wouldn't hate so I could just get it over with and pop the damn question already?

Her eyes fluttered as if she might start to cry.

I blinked. Shit, now how do I fix *this* mess that my previous lie had just created?

"Jordan! Please tell me what's going on. I—"

My phone rang. April blinked and recrossed her arms, her beautiful blue eyes shooting daggers right through me.

It was Anna. I knew it had to be her. Asking why she'd only gotten half a text that didn't make any sense.

I blinked.

April's eyes narrowed. They dared me to answer.

The sky outside our window was getting darker and darker... closing time.

*Fuck.* "Let me just get this—"

Her eyes bulged, incredulous. "Don't you fucking—"

Yeah, I fucking dared.

I answered it.

She gasped, and I turned my back, on her, heading into the bathroom. "Yeah, hi. Sorry about that text." I shut the door and briefly—quietly—told Anna I needed her to take me around to a decent jewelry store—and quickly.

My girl was about to lose her shit, and that was going to be even messier to clean up than this mess I'd already created.

I bolted from the bathroom, my arm up in preparation. As I knew she would, she got a couple shots off—pillows came right at me. Usually when she was throwing stuff in the bedroom, it was playful—or foreplay.

But this was straight-up, flat-out anger. "I promise I'll explain everything when I get back!" I shouted as I bolted from the room. I could have sworn I saw her pick up the fireplace poker out of the corner of my eye, so I hastened my departure.

Twenty minutes later, after meeting Anna at the jeweler— she'd asked them to keep it open for me with the promise of a sure sale—I texted April and asked her to meet me in the solarium of the mansion after dinner.

The time for fancy uber epic proposals was over. I just needed to get this shit done already, while I still had a girlfriend to propose to.

# Chapter 27
## *April*

THIS WAS IT. I'D HAD ENOUGH.

He'd once liked comparing me to Disney princesses. When we were dating, I was Snow White. Well this buckaroo was about to feel the cold sting of Snow White transforming into Elsa the Ice Queen. It was time to start Operation Freeze Out. I was actually currently contemplating freezing out certain parts of his body of which he thought very highly.

I'd never in a thousand years have thought that Jordan would cheat, given his own history with a fiancée who'd cheated on him, but what else could explain this? Before we'd become a couple, he'd been a perpetual hound-dog in rut, screwing everything in a skirt. Honestly, how could I have presumed to tame such a beast?

I was this-close to packing up my shit and heading out early when I rounded a corner to the dining room and almost ran into the culprit herself. Anna was setting up the table for the caterers in the morning and unloading a basket.

Jordan had texted me to meet him after dinner, but he still wasn't back, and we'd finished eating an hour ago. He'd gone off to meet *her*, I was almost certain. I hadn't heard all of the phone conversation in the bathroom but I had heard him say her name.

I wanted to cry and find my girl squad for sympathy. But here I was, alone in the dining room with *her* instead. My eyes narrowed in on Anna like the scope on a sniper rifle, ready to pick her off.

Elsa the Ice Queen could just as easily set her sights on the other woman as she could fantasize about freeze-drying certain male appendages, so there was that!

"Oh, hello April. I was just—"

"You need to back off." My spine stiffened and I folded my arms over my chest, shoulders squared.

She blinked.

Summoning my most badass cowgirl, hand on hips, I narrowed my eyes at her. "My prized bull doesn't graze in other pastures. And I don't take kindly to rustlers."

The front door opened and slammed. Anna stared at me like I was insane. "Are you...um... do you own a ranch?"

The nerve of her standing there acting all innocent and like she didn't understand what I was trying to say. I raised my finger to her. "Listen, beotch—"

Footsteps approached quickly and just before I might have lunged to get in this woman's face, I felt hands settle on my shoulders. Big hands. Strong hands.

My Beast's hands.

"April, let's go have that talk."

Anna's eyes raised from looking at me to meeting Jordan's gaze, and I went supernova. "Don't even look at him, lady! He's—"

But Jordan was pulling me away toward the solarium before I could finish. It was quiet in there, and it was dark. Jordan flipped on just one of the lights so that it was still kind of dim.

My throat was tight and my heart raced. Shit. Was this it? Was he going to admit to me that my worst suspicions were actually true?

I shrugged off his arm and pulled away, hugging myself, suddenly cold. Then, I turned on him. "I want the truth and I want it *now*. Stop with the bullshit."

He froze and we held a stare. Tension snapped between us and I felt my back go stiff. Was I about to get some glib, slick presentation of lies? Or was he going to confess? Were we about to break up? My stomach bottomed out.

*Oh God, no.* I sucked in a breath and held it.

Then he blinked and bent down.

Way down. Like he was about to faint or something.

"Jordan—!" I reached out a hand—as if I'd have the strength to steady him if he fell over.

Instead, he was on a knee, holding out a box—a jewelry box. Not the blue Tiffany one. This one was black, and there, nestled against dark blue velvet was a very traditional, brilliant-cut diamond in white gold. Classy. The stone winked at me in the low light.

I blinked. Confused. What the...?

"April, will you—"

My hands shot out in front of me, fingers spread wide. "Stop it! That isn't funny."

His brows scrunched together. "It's not supposed to be funny."

"Stop joking around!"

His brows now climbed his forehead. "I'm not doing that, either..."

I shook my head. "Then what...what is this?"

He threw a long glance out the corner of his eyes like a frightened animal, as if to figure out whether or not I was setting a trap for him.

"What does it look like? It's a marriage proposal."

What the... what? The air rushed out of my lungs as if I'd been punched. "Oh Jordan! What did you do?"

He cocked his head, truly puzzled. "Huh?"

"Did you—and her—Anna—did you two—did...?"

He shot to his feet and all but dropped that ring trying to get to me as I took a step backward. He had his hands on my arms.

"April! April... babe. No. *No*. Why would you think that?"

I gestured with a long sweep of my arm. "You've been sneaking off to talk to her, and she's all over you like cheap lycra and—and—the texting and the phone calls and—"

"No, no....April. She was helping me plan it all."

I shook my head. "Plan? What do you mean *plan*?"

He rolled his eyes and sighed. "I didn't want to ask you like this. I wanted it to be... I wanted it to be huge, *epic*, memorable--something you could brag about to your friends. I wanted—a gondola ride over the valley where I sink to a knee and ask you in between the mountains or... or... a hot air balloon or a castle in Europe. I wanted it to make you happy. Because I know you really want it."

I breathed, listened, breathed again. Let his words sink in as he spoke to me.

"But—but you don't want to get married. That's why I tease you about it."

Now it was his turn to hesitate, breathe, blink—and then frown. "What?"

"I tease you because it's funny. Not because I'm dying to get married."

Another long pause while he stared at me, possibly to assess whether or not I was serious. "Really?"

I nodded. "Yes, really. I'm not dying to get married. But I am always dying to make you squirm, and joking about marriage and weddings and all that is low-hanging fruit when it comes to freaking you out!"

Suddenly his entire body when slack as if from great relief. He reached a hand up and ran it through his hair. "I wanted this because I thought it would make you happy."

"Oh, Beast..." I walked up to him and pulled him into my arms. "That's not the reason to ask me. Ask me because it's what *you* want."

His arms came around me, encircling my shoulders and pulling me against his hard, broad chest. I inhaled his scent, closing my eyes. "I do want it. I mean I will want it. I..."

"You're not ready." I cleared my throat and cocked my head to look up at him. "And neither am I."

"You thought I was cheating—or going to cheat—with Anna. You're not secure in our relationship."

"A ring is not the solution to *that* either." I swallowed. "Honestly, it was the very first time in the two years we've been together that I've ever gotten paranoid. You were just acting so weird. I thought... Don't laugh, but I actually thought my stupid marriage jokes scared you off, and you just wanted to go back to your old hound dog days."

He blew out a breath and laughed, his arms tightening me against him. "Oh jeez, babe. I wouldn't go back to those days if you paid me. I mean, they were fun and all but..."

"But you outgrew that?"

He leaned down and kissed the top of my head. "Yes. Anna might have been the type I'd hit on for a good roll in the hay in my past. But that's not me anymore. And I'm not even the least bit tempted. When I want to hold someone, it's you I want to hold. When I want to touch someone and feel her touch me, that person is you. When I want to come home after a tough day at work and talk to someone—that's you, too."

I buried my face in his chest again to hide the tears that were prickling behind my eyes. But they overflowed, and I was shaking. It didn't take him long to realize it.

"April—babe. Why are you crying?"

"I feel terrible."

He reached down and took my chin in his big hand and lifted my face so he could look down into it. "It's okay. Sometimes I get a little crazy jealous too. I just don't tell you about it. Like when we're out and a guy gets a little too interested in checking out your perfect ass or amazing rack. Or when someone at the office gets flirty with you. Sometimes I get a little scared you might meet some guy in one of your MBA classes."

I laughed, and because my nose was now plugged with tears, it came out as a snort.

He laughed. "Now you sound like Mia."

"I'm sorry I doubted you," I whispered.

He reached down and dried my tears. "As long as you weren't going to leave my ass, then we're good."

I bit my lip guiltily. "I think I might have considered it for about five minutes. But that's because I thought you were into her."

He shook his head. "Nope. I'm into a much much hotter chick. The hottest. I'm pretty damn obsessed."

My eyes closed, tingles of pleasure trickling down my shoulders and back just from his words. "I love you."

"I love you, babe. Always." He reached up and pulled some hair out of my face, tucking it back behind my ear. "And now I'm going to need your help."

"For what?"

"You need you to help me figure out what the hell I'm going to do with two engagement rings."

I laughed, my eyes squeezing closed. "Oh my god, that first one was yours too? The one you said was William's?"

"I swear to god it's the first time I've ever lied to you."

"I guess it was for a good cause. But honestly, I want you to understand something. I don't need fancy. I don't need flashy and something to brag about. I've already got the best thing to brag about—my hot surfer-dude genius CFO boyfriend who makes all other guys look like wannabes. I already brag about you. I have no shame about that either. I don't need some obnoxious over-the-top engagement story. I don't need the gaudiest gigantic rock you can find. I want to go with you, when we know the time is right for both of us, and pick out our rings side-by-side. When both of us are certain that will make us happy, okay?"

He bent down and kissed my forehead again. "That sounds perfect to me."

I sniffed again really loud. "I need to blow my nose."

He turned and scanned room around us. "I don't see any tissue here. Let me go find you something."

"There's tissue in our room. Let's just go grab it there. I'll blow my nose and then…if you're a good boy, I might consider blowing something else…" I waggled my brows up at him.

"Tissues it is. As soon as humanly possible."

He grabbed my hand and lead me back to our room at such a fast walk that I practically had to run to keep up with him.

My beast… he'd never change in that respect.

# Chapter 28
## WILLIAM

"D UDE, YOU GOTTA TELL HER..."

"I've already told her, and nothing has changed since I did." I argue back at Lucas. Normally I'd be discussing this with my cousin or Jordan. But Jordan annoyed me by trying to get me to lie to his girlfriend about an engagement ring. And Adam is so preoccupied with whatever he's trying to accomplish with Mia that he's useless. But I had to ask someone's opinion.

We're sitting on the covered back porch—the solarium—at a table looking out at the view and drinking warm winter drinks. Lucas has a latte and I have hot chocolate.

Lucas blinks, cocks his head at me, as if expecting me to say more. I just look back at him.

"I mean, you've told her....once?"

I make a gesture. "More than once, actually. I even said it in her native language. In a church. That should be enough."

Lucas lets out a little snort and shakes his head. "It's never enough. They like to hear it. A lot. It's reassuring. I mean... she says it to you, right?"

I shrug. "She says a lot of things to me that are repetitive and unnecessary—"

Lucas straightens and holds up a hand. "Whoa, who said that saying *I love you* isn't necessary?"

"*I* say that repeating yourself isn't necessary. She's aware that I have a good memory. She doesn't have to keep reminding me, especially of a fact as important as that."

Lucas laughs. "She's not just saying it for you, though. She's saying it for herself, too. It's how she expresses herself."

I frown and set down my now-empty mug, considering whether I should fix a third cup of hot chocolate. Between that and the Bosnian cookies, I'll have to work out harder when I come home from vacation. "You mean, she has to remind herself that she loves me? I thought she had a good memory."

Lucas studies me for a moment, rubbing his jaw. "It's… it's like putting a lifeline out there for your partner, you know? Life can get a little messy, a little stormy. You have a bad day at work, her car broke down. Things didn't go well at school. Maybe you even snapped at each other because you were tired or hungry or whatever. But even when you aren't feeling great about each other—angry or irritated, that is always there. It's a constant. Like the life-saver on a boat. You throw out that *I love you* to remind yourself and your partner that you are there for them in the storm. They aren't alone."

I frown. He's making an analogy, and I'm typically not good at following those, but I think I grasp what he's trying to say. "But those are just words. What do they do, really? I'd rather show my love with actions."

"As long as she understands that's what you're doing with your actions, right? You need to be on the same page—I mean, speak the same language." Lucas nodded, considering. "It's true that there are a lot of ways to show your love, too. Purposely losing a skiing race might be one I need to consider…" he says with a grin that I don't fully understand.

*Speak the same language.* Yes, we both speak English. But I think Lucas is making another analogy. My actions are my way of showing her my love, but if she doesn't understand that, then she won't feel what I'm trying to tell her when I fetch her a drink without asking, when I help her build a bulletin board for her classroom or when I make her a carrying case for her Tarot cards. I use my hands to tell her how I feel.

That makes it sound like it's about sex.

I'm glad I've had this talk with Lucas. I'd been skeptical at first, since I didn't know him as well as Adam and Jordan, but so far, he's scored much higher on the quality of his advice versus the other two.

With this new information, I've come to a decision. Whether or not I'm finished with it, I need to show her the project I've been working on.

She needs that assurance.

So I fix more hot chocolate—this time, two mugs, and carry them, with my sketchpad under my arm, into the other room. I find her there, looking at her phone and ask if she'll join me in the upstairs library.

"Hey, Wil. Yeah, sure. Lucas and Kat have their ski race in a little while… and tonight it's New Years. Have you decided what you want to do?"

I blink. "Well, I'll leave the decision up to you."

She falls in behind me as we climb the stairs. "And if I want to go out to a public gathering, dancing and partying until midnight?"

I hesitate, considering. It sounds like something I'd completely dislike. But I'd do it, if that's what she wanted. I just wouldn't enjoy myself, and then I'd probably add it to my *never again* list.

"I'm teasing. Just go..."

I resume climbing and we enter the library. I set the mugs on the coffee table and she grins. "Thanks for the chocolate, but I'm not going to be able to fit in these jeans much longer if you keep making it for me. Then you'll regret it."

I blink, settling down on the couch. "It wouldn't matter to me if you gained weight, as long as you stayed healthy. It wouldn't change how I feel..."

Jenna hesitates, her mug halfway to her mouth before she turns to me. "And... and how is it that you feel?"

I stare at her for a long moment. "It's not obvious?"

She ducks her head, sips from the mug, and then replaces it on the coffee table. "Well, sometimes, you know, I like to be reminded."

"Yes, I think I understand."

Her pale blue eyes flew up to meet mine, eyebrows raising a bit. "You do?"

I pull out my sketchbook and set it down between us on the couch.

"You wanted me to say the words and I didn't understand how important they were for you to hear. But when you made that scarf for me—"

"The scratchy one with all the flaws?"

I reached out and took her hand. " Yes, it's flawed and scratchy. But it also kept me warm when I was cold and miserable. You made it with these beautiful hands. Just for me.

Whenever I wear it, I think about all it took for you to make it. And when you gave it to me on Christmas—even though it wasn't done, and it had missing stitches—it made me feel good inside. That you'd learned this new skill and the first thing you thought to make was something for me."

She blinked, her eyes suddenly going rounder.

I cleared my throat and kept talking. "And so, I had the thought to use my hands to make something for you. It's not a new skill but I didn't have the time to learn something new. But since you like my drawings…" I pushed the sketchpad toward her. "Open it up."

She reached out, took it, and did as I asked. I watched her face as she looked at the first page—a sketch of a small cottage amid a familiar backdrop, a piece of land we'd recently bought. Three acres in the Cuyamaca mountains right beside the lake in San Diego county. Our plan is to someday build a cottage there and live sustainably. It was her dream, and we were already acquiring skills to learn how to do it.

Her eyes landed on the sketch, a hand reached out to the page as she let out a long breath. "Oh, William… our cottage! You've drawn it."

"Turn the page."

And she did. The sketches showed the cottage from every angle, just as we'd discussed. We'd actually spent many hours talking about it. She wants a herd of goats and to make  her own cheese and soap. I want a sprawling vegetable garden and, of course, a forge and art studio. We'd even spent time out there, camping in a tent. While we were there, we'd walk around the property and talk about what we wanted to put and where we'd put it.

She continued to page through the sketches of the outside from different angles, and then she got to the page with the interiors. She put her thin, delicate fingertips to her mouth. "It's beautiful. I didn't even have the imagination to dream this up, but you've translated what we've talked about so beautifully. Oh, Wil, all that time you were working on your sketches, *this* was what you were doing. What an amazing gift."

I look down, suddenly aware that my time spent on this had mad her sad. "I'm sorry that working on it was making you upset."

She shook her head. "It's—it's all right. I understand, now. You wanted to surprise me."

"I don't know if I like surprising people anymore. It means I have to lie or be secretive until the time is right." I shake my head. "I don't think it's worth it."

She laughs and lifts her eyes to mine, her smile growing wider. She reached her hand out and smoothed it across my cheek. "In this case, it was definitely worth it. Thank you."

I take her hand from my cheek and bring it to my mouth, kissing it. "I know I don't tell you as often as you'd want, but I love you. I'll try to say it more."

She smiled and a silvery tear streams from her eye. I still don't understand why, but I know that sometimes Jenna cries when she's happy, so I'm not concerned. "I think I just understood something, too. That you *do* tell me often. Just not with words."

I squeeze her hand, at once happy and also relieved that she understands me.

She sets the pad aside and scoots herself close to me. In seconds, her arms are locked around my neck. We're kissing and holding each other, and I've pulled her so tightly against me that it's hard for either of us to breathe.

There's this feeling inside, a tightness in my chest. I know it's not the case, but it feels like my heart is too big inside of there. I guess that's where the sentiment came from—that love is felt in the heart.

But it's just a sentiment. Because I feel my love for Jenna all over my body, everywhere.

And as I kiss her and smell her sweetness and hold her close, I know that I'll never get tired of telling her I love her, whether it's with my words or with my hands, with the things I make or what I do for her.

And I know that it's the same for her.

And that even though sometimes life feels uncomfortable, uncertain—*stormy,* to use Lucas's metaphor—we'll be each other's lifeline. Each other's anchor.

It makes me feel safe.

# CHAPTER 29
## KATYA

YOU'VE MADE SOME DUMBASS DECISIONS IN YOUR LIFE, *Katharina Rose Ellis, but this might be the dumbest one of all.*

My legs were dangling from the chair lift and I couldn't pull my eyes off my skis, which wobbled back and forth as I kicked them nervously. I half wished one of them would fall off my boot, down, down, down into the snow. *Poof*, never to be seen again and then—whoops!—no crazy-ass ski race!

Beside me, Lucas gripped his side of the chair in response to the wobbling and turned to me as a wind kicked up.

"Jesus, Kat, what are you trying to do, dump us off the chair?"

"What, you're such an expert with skiing, why would you be afraid of that?"

"Because I don't fly?" He shrugged. "What's the matter, trying to take out the competition?"

The ski lift stopped momentarily, right when we reached the highest point. The wind kicked up, and a flurry of ice and flakes rose on the breeze, stinging my eyes. I still refused to lower my goggles.

I blew out a breath and shook my head, muttering, "This competition is so lame."

"What?"

"I said, *This competition is so lame!*" This time I yelled it. I may have started an avalanche down a hidden canyon somewhere nearby. But damn it, I was frustrated.

"About time you realized that."

I arched a brow at him. "Maybe you should have chimed in when Jordan came up with the stupid idea."

He gestured with open hands. "Because I thought you wanted it, too. You know, since you're always looking for a reason to compete with me."

"People who live in glass houses shouldn't challenge their wife to a ski race!"

"Um, *what?*"

"We compete about everything. It's not just me, is it? You do it, too."

He shook his head. "I don't—"

"Then why don't you tell me why you've been going to such pains to keep your work troubles a secret from me? Maybe you don't want me to find out because somehow that means I'm winning because I like my new job?"

His face clouded and he looked away.

"See? Proof that we both do it," I concluded, taking his lack of denial for agreement.

He looked back at me. The lift still hadn't started up again and I had no way to tell what was holding it up. Maybe someone had fallen when descending? Didn't bode well for *us*.

I turned to him and raised my brows, expecting him to speak.

"Why the hell *are* we doing this?" he finally asked.

"It's not my fault!" I squeaked. "Jordan started it."

"Fucking Jordan." He ground out between clenched teeth.

Another beat passed and the lift jerked to a start again. We both burst out laughing at the same time.

I shook my head. "Too bad he's not here or I'd kick his ass with my ski boots on."

"I'd dump him headfirst into the snow," Lucas contributed.

"I can't believe he even put us up to this."

"And twisted our arms to get us to perform, like dancing monkeys to place bets on. He wanted us to do it on a black diamond run, too. Can you imagine?"

"Fucking Jordan!" I yelled so loud that it echoed across the valley. Another beat passed and we were quiet. I glanced at him out of the corner of my eye. "Just 'cause he put us up to this doesn't mean we have to do it."

He sighed and fixed his knit beanie on top of his head. "I feel obligated. The boss is watching now."

I peered at him out of the corner of my eye. "Is work going *that* badly? And why didn't you tell me? Maybe I could help."

He heaved a long sigh and shook his head. "Okay I confess. I didn't want to tell you about the bullshit I'm dealing with because you're doing amazing at your new job and I'm not doing that great at mine."

I looked at him like he was an alien. "But... both Jordan and Adam said you're doing a great job."

Lucas unconsciously looked toward the platform where all our friends stood perched at a perfect vantage point to watch the beginning of our race. Right now, they were stuffed behind the trees and we couldn't see them. "Because they don't know. I'm struggling with two of my employees who are at each other's throats and threatening to quit every other day if I don't fire the other one."

I threw my husband a look. "Yeah, I'm sure they've *never* had to deal with childish employees, ever."

He blinked a few times. "You… have a good point."

"I do have them sometimes." I sent him a self-satisfied smile.

He took in a deep breath and sighed heavily, his breath billowing out like a cloud. "Man, that felt good to finally confess."

I shot him a slightly guilty look and swallowed. "I have something to confess, too."

He turned to me expectantly.

I bit my lip. "I may have…exaggerated my skiing abilities." He blinked, and then there was a sudden and noticeable change in his body language. His shoulders slumped. Was that relief? I cleared my throat. "You should know by now that I'm ninety percent bravado, five-percent pluck and a three percent lucky."

"And the other two percent?"

I swallowed, studying the slope ahead under our chair as we climbed higher. "That's the crazy."

"You're *not* crazy, Kat."

"I got us into this race, didn't I?"

He shook his head vehemently. "No, we just agreed that Jordan did it."

I laughed. "Oh, yeah."

"I think we're both suffering from a big misunderstanding."

I bit my lip. "I was planning to tell you that first night in the diner after dinner. But the whole thing just blew so far out of proportion. Everyone's stupid Canadian jokes were making me fed up, so I exaggerated my skills. *A lot.* And then Jordan baited you—"

"Adam was right there. I wasn't going to back down in front of my boss."

I tucked my head down. "Why *are* we always competing with each other?"

He shrugged helplessly. "Maybe because of how our relationship started out? I've been complicit in it too...."

We both turned to look ahead. The chair was approaching the top of the slope and it was time to slide off. "We're gamers. Of course we're competitive. Just... I wish it didn't have to be with everything, you know? Ultimately, we're on the same team."

As the slope rose to meet us, we both descended and headed, side-by-side toward the beginning point of the intermediate run. From the distance, above us on the slope, came the distant sounds of cheering and calling. Our heads both pointed up, up, up 'til we caught sight of them on the observation area. A cluster of our friends all bundled up and madly waving.

Lucas gave a long, forlorn sigh.

"I think it's time for the dancing monkeys to rebel," I said.

His brows rose almost to the brim of his knit cap. "Excuse me?"

"Let's refuse to race. We'll just go down at our own pace."

His eyes narrowed. "This isn't some trick so you'll beat me, is it?"

I shook my head. "I'm dead serious. Besides, you're a way better skier than I am. I wouldn't have a chance. I'm admitting that now. Out loud."

His expression grew sheepish. "Then I have another confession to make..."

"Oh?"

"I ski like shit. Rich kid or no. European winter vacations or no, it's never been my thing."

I lost it, right there on the slope. I started laughing so hard, even as people pushed past us to start their run. "Oh my god, we're such dorks. Let's get off this mountain and go play some Steep on the PlayStation. Good *healthy* competition."

His grin widened. "Only problem is that the only way off this mountain is down. But we can always go together."

"I'd suggest holding hands, but Imma need both my poles for balance. However, let's make a pact not to laugh at each other, okay?"

"Sounds good to me. Let's just make this a leisurely trip down the mountain on our way to sitting cozy by the fire and pretending to ski on a console game."

Together we flashed a thumbs up at our friends who watched from above. Then, with a "Here goes nothin'," we pushed ourselves down the hill.

Easy peasy, lemon squeezy, right?

Well… not exactly.

# CHAPTER 30
## *LUCAS*

NEW YEAR'S EVE DAY IN A CANADIAN EMERGENCY ROOM waiting for results on my wife's x-rays was not my idea of a good time. Yes indeed… the last day of the year and I'd ended up putting my wife in the hospital.

I shuddered to think of what might have happened if we'd *actually* been racing. It could have been so much worse, but still, it was bad. I sat up, paced in a circle, sat back down, fiddled with my wedding ring. I couldn't sit still, and I wouldn't rest easy until Kat was back from radiology.

"Sit down, man, you're making me nervous."

I turned an acid eye toward Jordan. "Oh, well, excuse me. It's just my wife in there with God knows how many broken bones…" I gestured wildly with my arm in the direction they'd wheeled her twenty minutes before.

Jordan blinked and cast a concerned glance in the same direction. "She's all right. I mean, she's gotta be all right. Kat's a tough girl, right? Really tough."

We'd been rushed down the mountain on a snowmobile to the first aid station at the bottom where she'd been checked out on the spot.

She hadn't hit her head, but her ankle was painful and swelling like a balloon. And there was no putting weight on it.

I just hoped she hadn't fractured anything. Damn it. That would be painful and a long recovery, and since it was her ankle, possible surgery depending on how bad it was.

My stomach knotted and I ran a hand through my hair.

At least Jordan had the decency to look worried.

The nurse showed up to tell us that Kat was back in the examining room. The doctor was looking at her X-rays and would be in shortly. I shot out of my chair to follow her.

Jordan did the exact same thing.

He'd come with us while the rest of the group waited back at the mansion. Jordan had insisted, and though Mia might have been the more obvious choice in order to be with her best friend and offer medical advice if needed, Jordan wouldn't hear of it.

I turned to him. "Haven't you done enough?"

"Man, I just want to make sure she's all right so I can text everyone and give them some news. Hopefully good news." He looked stricken. Almost guilty. *Good.* It was his big ol' mouth that had gotten us into this in the first place.

When we got into the room, Kat was doubled over and moaning, crying.

Holy Shit.

"It hurts. It hurts so much. Damn. Ohhhh." When I went to her, she all but fell into my arms from the top of the examination table and I wrapped them around her tightly.

"Shh. I'm sorry. I'm so sorry."

"Jordan is the one who should be sorry!" she half shouted. Fuck. It must *really* hurt because I had never seen her like this. I mean, she cried, of course. Once in a while. For emotional reasons. But she seemed to tolerate pain well under normal circumstance. This must have been real agony.

"Tell him to go away. I don't even want to look at him."

I shot Jordan a death glare over my wife's head.

Jordan threw his hands up. "I'm going. I'm going I just wanted to say I'm so sorry, Kat. I take full responsibility. It was totally stupid to pit you two against each other, and I really feel like shit. Please can I—"

"Gooooo!" she howled into my chest, and with a sigh of resignation, he backed up. His gaze met mine and his hands were up helplessly.

Then he turned and was gone.

A minute later, Kat asked me if he was gone and I reassured her that he was.

Then she pushed away and straightened. "Good, because I have no idea how much longer I could have kept that up."

I blinked and stared into Kat's face. Clear eyes, no hint of crying whatsoever. "What?"

"Oh, he deserved it. Do not even tell me you think he didn't deserve a little guilt trip."

I scratched my forehead, puzzled. "You had *me* going there, too."

She waved a hand. "Yeah, sorry. You were collateral damage. I just want him to stew on that for a while."

I shook my head. "So... you aren't in pain?"

She shook her head. "They shot me up with something before they took me to radiology. I don't feel a damn thing. But Jordan doesn't need to know that. Maybe I can get a billionaire to wait on me hand and foot for the rest of the time we're here. Maybe I'll make him dress up in something funny or figure out some other way to humiliate him."

My lips thinned. "Well as funny as the idea of all that is, Jordan is still technically my boss."

Her eyes widened. "Oooh I know, maybe he'll give you a raise to appease his guilt!"

I laughed. Not long after, the doctor came in to inform us that it was just a severe sprain and we were discharged shortly thereafter. I, of course, had to hear all about the superiority of Canadian health care from my Canadian wife. She wasn't wrong, after all.

Jordan hardly said anything to us on the way back to the mansion, sufficiently cowed. Eventually I'd clue him in.

He had huge bouquet of flowers waiting for her in our room. A gigantic "I'm sorry" mylar balloon floated above it near the ceiling. Kat broke up into hysterics the minute I carried her through the doorway and she saw it.

"I'm going to ask Anna to get a gigantic balloon of a moose with a maple leaf on it for him and tell him he has to fly home with it tied to his wrist like a four-year-old."

And we had fun dreaming up other possible humiliations for Jordan.

A few hours later, Mia and Adam stopped to say goodbye and check on her on their way out the door for their special overnight stay in a secluded location.

And even I couldn't help but notice how amazing they looked in their finest attire. Adam was actually wearing a dark suit with a gray tie and Mia had on a short royal blue dress made of crushed velvet paired with shiny black heels.

Wow.

Kat's eyes widened. "Mia! No fair! You have all the glam, and I have none, and it's New Year's Eve. You're going to go dancing tonight, aren't you? And here I am with my ankle the size of a rugby ball." She sighed and then gave her friend a lopsided smile. "You're so beautiful! Happy one-year anniversary, you two!"

Mia bent and gave her a hug. Adam asked how she was doing, bent, and kissed her on the cheek. Neither of them would leave until we reassured them that we had everything we needed. Copious ice packs. Her filled prescription bottle. And doctor's orders to keep her off her feet and her injured ankle elevated.

Only then was Mia satisfied, and with some relief, Adam took her by the hand and led her away. On their way out the front door, the rest of our friends lined up to wish them a happy anniversary and send them on their way.

And they were off.

And… we were alone in our room.

My wife, despite her injury and supposed lack of glam, was looking incredibly fetching with her slightly loopy lopsided smile, her disheveled flame hair and her cheerful eyes.

"Come here. You are supposed to be at my beck and call, right? So I'm officially becking and calling you."

"I think it's beckoning," I corrected as I approached her.

Her blue eyes gleamed and she licked her lips. "Mmm. I love it when you speak private school rich boy to me."

"I could do other things that you love even more."

"As long as I don't have to be too athletic or use my foot, I'm all in."

I laughed. "Unless you are thinking of some weird-ass position I'm not familiar with, then no foot action necessary."

With a lot of laughs and even more kisses, I pulled her against me, hastily unbuttoning the front of her nightshirt. Once it fell away and her prefect naked breasts were revealed I sucked in a gasp of arousal. "Oh, you have no idea how thankful I am that you didn't sprain your boobs."

She fell back flat against her pillow laughing deep from her gut. "Well thank God you didn't sprain your mouth."

"Yeah let me show you exactly how healthy my mouth is feeling right now..."

And I covered very inch of her body I could reach with kisses. No competition here. Just good old-fashioned teamwork. Rewarded in orgasms.

# CHAPTER 31
## *JENNA*

"**W**ILLIAM," I CALLED OUT, DRAGGING MY handsome boyfriend's attention away from still more of his sketching in the reading nook. He'd been as concerned about Kat's welfare as the rest of us, but he'd also been beyond annoyed about having to stand out in the cold to watch the race—such as it was.

He'd hardly left the fireside since we'd returned to the house. I was afraid my sweetie had had enough of the cold weather, the mountains, and the snow and was ready to get back to sunny Southern California. And while the weather wasn't exactly warm at home by our standards, it was practically tropical next to these high altitude and high latitude winter temperatures.

Which made me smile all the more when I thought of the surprise I'd been cooking up for the past couple hours while William warmed up by the fire and perfected his sketches.

"I need you to take a trip with me."

He looked up from his sketchbook, puzzled. I was taking a risk of frustrating him by being too figurative, but he'd catch on quickly enough. It wasn't like I was about to prolong it.

"What? When?"

I climbed the three steps up to the elevated nook and took a last look at the mountains as the dusk was coming in, turning the skies purple and blue. So beautiful… "We're going to the tropics. Right now."

He blinked at me. "What?"

I smiled and held out both my hands for him to take. "Put the book down and come with me, please!"

With a deep sigh, as if I had just assigned a million chores for him to do, he complied and put his pencil and book aside. Then he stood and took one of my hands. "I'm sure I'll understand soon because I have no idea what you're talking about right now."

I squeezed his hand gently and tugged him along with me. "Oh, you'll understand very quickly."

Then I led him into the solarium where I'd pulled the wide, tall curtains against the cold wintery backdrop. The huge, mounted television on the far wall was streaming a video I'd found on YouTube showing a tropical shore and swaying palm trees. Polynesian music quietly streamed in through the streamers. I'd cranked the two restaurant-style propane heaters up to full blast to make it nice and warm.

William stopped beside me and scanned the room, taking it all in. I took advantage of his distraction to grab my little creations off a nearby table. The house had been filled with fresh flower arrangements when we'd arrived, and when I got my idea earlier, I'd decided to repurpose some of those gorgeous flowers into makeshift flower crowns. They hardly looked authentic, but they'd do in a pinch. I put one on my head and picked up the other one for him.

This might be tricky. He typically didn't like things on his head—hats and the like--but I could always grab a little string and turn it into an ugly lei instead.

To my surprise, William studied the crown on my head for a long moment before quietly dipping his head and giving me silent permission to put the crown on his head. He adjusted it once his head raised.

"So we're imagining ourselves in some tropical location?"

"French Polynesia! Look. We have dinner—I ordered some Hawaiian food—Kalua style pork and rice. And there's a tray of fresh fruit, even some pineapple. The concierge got it all arranged for me when I'd called her earlier. Isn't that cool?"

"No, it's not cool. It's warm." He punctuated his statement with a smile. Only William could get away with a joke like that, and I laughed, truly meaning it.

"I also made us some tropical drinks, and look—there's a big towel spread out next to the jacuzzi. So we can enjoy our beach luau."

"I don't believe they do luau in French Poly—"

"William, just roll with it, please? We're pretending."

He blinked and a slow smile crept onto his face. "Okay. But can I pretend to sit on the beach and watch you doing a special Polynesian dance?"

My eyes widened. I had no idea how to dance that style, but I could always improvise. So he settled himself down on the towel and I twirled and moved my hips a little—I had taken some belly dance classes, so I supposed it was a tiny bit like that, anyway. I moved my arms through the air like I'd seen Polynesian dancers do before.

When I was done, I curtsied, and William clapped. Then I joined him on the towel.

"How was that?"

"I think French Polynesia is amazing. Much better than the cold snow and ice."

I smiled and landed a big kiss on his mouth. "Good."

"Since we're here in French Polynesia, I have something special to say to you."

I picked up an empty plate and began to fill it for him. "Oh? What is that?"

"*Je t'aime.* It means—"

"I love you. In French! Now you know how to say it in three languages—English, Bosnian and French."

He shook his head. "I'm at fifteen so far and hope to add another twenty before we get home."

My eyes bulged. "What?"

"You like to hear the words, but I figured it might get boring for me to say the same thing over and over again, so I'm going to learn different ways to say it." Then, as if to illustrate his point, he signed something to me in what I could only assume was American Sign Language. And I could only assume it was *I love you.*

*Oh William!* I could look the world over and never ever find someone as unique and amazing and so incredible.

I set the plate down and threw my arms around his neck. Our mouths met in a delicious, heated kiss. "Do you mind if your dinner gets a little cold?"

He pulled me tightly against him. "There's always the microwave."

Then he leaned back on the towel, pulling me with him and, laughing, I went.

French Polynesia was a wonderful place to celebrate New Year's Eve.

# CHAPTER 32
## *HEATH*

WELL AFTER THE CRAZINESS OF KAT AND LUCAS'S SKI race—and the subsequent race to the Emergency Room—it was strange to think that things were finally calming down on New Year's Eve.

In my younger days, I'd spent some crazy-ass New Year's Eve celebrations getting blackout drunk or hooking up with some dude that looked much hotter with the beer goggles on than in the cold light of day. Some of those guys had actually ended up being coyote ugly—so bad you'd rather chew your own arm off than pull it out from under them and wake them up on your way out the door.

Oh the walks of shame on New Year's Day, head throbbing and mouth dry, from days of drinking past. And heavily medicating with the hair of the dog that bit you.

Shall auld acquaintance be forgot… and all that.

But this New Year's Eve? In the hot new ski resort with fresh meat everywhere, I found myself curiously uninterested, more into hanging out with friends and just enjoying the setting and their company. This was a new look for me.

Was I finally growing up?

I'd been hesitant to come when Mia had extended the invitation—the awkwardness of being the ninth wheel among the four couples and all that. But in the end, I was glad I came—if for no other reason than to hang out with three of my closest friends—Mia, Kat, and Adam—and their significant others and family members.

Not long after Kat's accident, after we'd all assured Mia that she'd be fine and we'd take care of her, we saw Adam and Mia off for their night alone together to celebrate their big anniversary.

April and Jordan left shortly afterwards, also dressed to the nines, to dine at some hotel in the village and join the festivities there. The rest were going to be homebodies.

Gregg, the concierge's assistant, had been trying to ask me out all week. I just wasn't into him. I was nice about it, and he took it like a grown-up. We ended up having an early dinner together at the same little diner where we'd all eaten at the beginning of the week.

The thought of more poutine sounded like a great idea to me.

We talked music—which was pretty much the only place our interests coincided—ate good food, had a beers. It wasn't a bad time. I came home a few hours before midnight.

As expected, the house was fairly quiet. I first ran into April and Jordan, already back early from their big night out, still dressed up all fancy. He wore a black designer suit perfectly tailored to his impressive physique, and she was in a classic little black dress that barely came past the top of her thighs, and shimmery high heels that looked like they cost more than I made in a month. And despite the rumors flying around our mansion for the past week, there was no diamond ring on her left hand. Jordan must have chickened out after all, if indeed there had been any truth to the gossip.

They had the music on and were dancing close, swaying against each other. Well, it was good to know I had some friends who could dance.

"Heath! Happy New Year. How was your date?" April said, from where her head was perched against her boyfriend's shoulder.

Jordan rested his head atop April's as they continued to sway together to the music. "Well he's back two hours before midnight, so I'm going to take a shot in the dark and say it wasn't the greatest."

"Naw, it wasn't a date. It was just poutine and beer at the diner. He's a nice enough guy, but...." I shrugged

"Not nice enough for you," April said, reaching out a hand to rest on my arm. She was clearly tipsy, well on her way to getting soused. Lucky Jordan. "Come—dance with us, Heath."

I put up my hand. "I'm good. I'm going to go peek in on Kat and see how she's doing then maybe pop some popcorn and watch a movie in the den."

"Knock yourself out, bro. Just don't drink alone," Jordan quipped.

I laughed. "Not planning on it. You two enjoy each other—I see that you're doing it already."

April turned her face into Jordan's chest and giggled a little bit. He steadied her against him, bringing his hand up to her head. He smoothed her hair and kissed the top of her head.

I left the living room and knocked on the door of Kat and Lucas's suite. It took them a minute before they called out for me to open the door. There was no small amount of giggling involved.

Oh boy, I'd interrupted something, obviously. I cracked the door open. "Hey you two, I'll let you get back to whatever you were up to—"

"Come in. I'm decent," Kat called.

I opened the door a bit. "But you weren't a minute ago, right?" She had the covers pulled all the way up to her neck but her wrapped foot peeked out from the covers, elevated on some pillows, as it was supposed to be. Lucas was fully clothed, though his shirt looked hastily pulled on. Well then.

"Happy New Year, Heath!" Kat called, a little too loudly, and raised her hand to wave frantically as if I were a mile away and she were trying to capture my attention.

"You haven't been drinking, have you?"

Lucas shook his head. "Nope, she's banned from alcohol because of the meds which, apparently, are compounding her natural silliness."

She laughed. "So my big take-away today? Never race your dude on a ski slope."

I smirked. "I'll take that under advisement should the issue ever arise, thanks. Anything I can get either of you? Water? Condoms?"

"Pfft. We don't need those, unless you are going to blow them up and make little balloon animals out of them," Kat said with another laugh.

Lucas leaned over and propped her foot back on the pillow. "The doc wants you to keep it elevated," he chided her mildly. Then he turned to me. "We're good. Thanks, Heath. You want to hang out in here and watch the countdown?"

I glanced at the TV. It wasn't even on. "Eh, I think I'm just gonna go chill in the den. You two seem to have plans for ringing in the new year that definitely don't involve me. Just tell Kat not to be too loud. We don't need to hear how much she's enjoying the pain meds—and you."

She grabbed a cushion and tossed it at me. And missed horribly. Testament to the loopiness from aforementioned pain meds.

"Ta ta. See you next year!"

I shut the door but I could hear her reply. "Oh, I get it! See you next year."

I laughed and shook my head. Hadn't had a drop to drink, and she was three sheets to the wind. Either they were about to both get lucky, or she was about to pass out for the next nine hours. Hard to tell which.

On my way to the kitchen for my movie snacks, I passed by the entrance to the solarium and saw that the TV screen and several lights were turned on. When I slipped in to turn them off, I noticed the couple sitting close and kissing on a towel spread out across the ground. They were under a big propane heat lamp right beside the bubbling jacuzzi, both wearing crowns of fresh flowers.

It was as warm as a summer day in here. The TV played an ambient video of a turquoise-blue ocean crashing onto powdery white sand, palm trees swaying in a breeze and the sun beating down.

Well... looked like someone'd had their fair share of the mountains and snow.

"Aloha," I said when they noticed me.

William frowned. "I don't think that's a Canadian greeting."

I waved to the TV, the lamp, the beach towel. "Clearly, you two aren't in Canada anymore."

Jenna smiled, reached into the jacuzzi, and sent me a splash that only hit me with a few warm droplets on my forehead. "We're in Tahiti!"

"Oh," I frowned, thinking. "*Bonjour*, then. That works for Canada *and* for Tahiti. See, William, I got you."

"We're just pretending to be in Tahiti," William provided unnecessarily. Strange explanation from a man who regularly dressed up in medieval armor and fought other men with a sword and shield.

But that was William for you—quirky, sometimes cantankerous, but a standup, pretty awesome guy.

Only a short while later, I couldn't say how I found myself outside in the snow-covered backyard after saying goodbye to Jenna and William and wishing them well on their tropical vacation. There'd been a whole lot of love and coupling going on inside that house and I'd needed to grab a break and collect my own thoughts.

Here I was with the cold biting my cheeks and my eyes watering—me hugging myself in my too-thin sweatshirt. The inadequate clothing was my own damn fault for jumping outside on impulse, I guess.

It was the last day of the year. I was in a house full of my closest friends, and yet... I was feeling philosophical and indulging in the need to be alone with the quiet and my thoughts. Reflecting on the future.

Still trying to figure out what I really wanted. I knew it certainly wasn't what I'd been living the past few years—parties, dating, wallowing in loneliness. It was time to move on. Time to grow, evolve. Time to shit or get off the fucking pot, already.

Shall auld acquaintance be forgot... no. *No* I couldn't forget. And I didn't want to.

I pulled out my phone and sent a simple, short text.

*I know it's been the new year for hours over there and you're probably sleeping it off but... just wanted to wish you a happy new year. I hope it's a good one for you.*

With a lump in my throat, I pressed send on the message to Connor before I chickened out. We were still in touch every so often, but it wasn't like it had been. And I'd been the one to pull away.

With a sigh, I blew out a breath, looking up at the glowing white mountains in the darkness and the field of stars twinkling above it. The crisp, cold air swirled around me, and I felt energized, alive.

Suddenly, all around me, noise.

Horns honked. People shouted and yelled. Some banged pots and pans, others blew air horns. And just above the resort in the valley—which I could watch from my perfect vantage point— fireworks flashed and cracked over Whistler village as the wind brought the distance sound of crowds cheering. It was midnight on the west coast.

I felt connected to the world and yet detached, an observer.

I had a good feeling about this year. About the things we'd all been through. Things were changing, yes, but not necessarily for the bad.

I turned my eyes toward the north, and caught the tiniest glimpse of green along the horizon, my first glimpse of the Northern Lights. I wondered if Adam and Mia could see them where they were, too.

Smiling, I silently wished them a happy anniversary, turned, and went inside.

# CHAPTER 33
## *ADAM*

I T WASN'T EVERY DAY THAT I WAS SERVED A FULL COURSE dinner prepared by a Michelin starred chef in a secluded mountain cabin and yet, here we were. And it most certainly wasn't every day that I celebrated my first wedding anniversary with my incredible wife either.

This was a once-in-a-lifetime day.

We'd been brought to this private retreat house via four-wheel drive, and then a horse-drawn sleigh across a smooth field of snow to an intimate, cozy cabin, all set up for us. Our meal was transported via snowmobile from a nearby kitchen where it was prepared.

And now we sat at an elegant table with a white damask tablecloth beside a fireplace as the short day faded into evening. A shy but friendly server was our only other company until she'd take her leave after bringing out dessert. And then, we'd be here, alone in the quiet, to spend the night together. No cell phones. No television. No Internet.

Just my beautiful wife and me.

A year ago today, we'd married on a tropical island in the Caribbean. This year, we were high in the snow-covered mountains. I half wondered where the second anniversary would take us. And the third? The tenth?

We'd have to get creative if we were setting the bar this high already.

Over appetizers—foie gras on toast with pear and caramelized onion—we made small talk. Discussed the accident with Kat on the slope and shared our concerns. Talked about the trip in general and mused over some of the more memorable moments—the phantom bear attack by the hot springs being our biggest laugh.

This week, we'd had some fun times, made some great memories, and even, after the years we'd been a couple, learned something new about each other.

We learned that there was never a finish line, never one fixed point that defined a happily ever after. That happily ever after was a thing to be guarded with vigilance, that took work and communication to maintain.

My god, were Emilia and I finally grown-ups?

We didn't end up really digging into the meat of matters until, ironically, we were cutting into our Beef Wellington paired with a delicious Bordeaux.

"So." I flicked my eyes up at her as I popped a piece of meat in my mouth and chewed.

She looked up from her plate. As always, she was stunning. Her long dark hair had been brushed out, draped across her shoulders in loose mahogany curls. Her tight blue dress was giving me all kinds of dirty thoughts about what I wanted after dessert. And the simple gold jewelry with the diamond pendant I'd given her for Christmas glistened at her throat in the candlelight.

She raised her brows to prompt me to continue. So I took a breath and did. "About that list…"

She rolled her eyes. "I burned the list. In our fireplace. I'm not afraid to admit that I enjoyed it."

I pointed to my temple. "It's all in here, baby."

She smiled big, revealing her even, white teeth. "Is that why you went frantically digging through the dirty laundry in search of it?"

I suppressed a smile. "The hard copy was a backup."

She gave me a wary look. "So what is it you want to say about the list before I politely change the subject?"

"I think a list is a good idea."

She frowned, her mouth crooking. "I thought we'd been over this…".

I wiped my mouth with a napkin and held up a hand. "Just hear me out. I didn't say *that* list. That list was the result of some random Google research I patched together in a panic within hours of having my phone cruelly seized—" Her brows raised in warning. "I mean, before I happily and voluntarily turned over my phone."

She tilted her head to the side, considering. "Okay and so…?"

"I think we should make our own list. You and I should sit down thoughtfully and work it out together. Our ways to reconnect. And once we've made it, we should commit to using it. As you said, our lifestyle right now is hectic, even if it is temporary. But you took that initial rate-your-marriage quiz for a reason, and I made that first infamous list for the same reason."

She cut her meat and then chewed, staring into the candlelight. Twin flames smoldered in her eyes as she mulled over the idea.

Then, once she'd swallowed, she nodded. "I like it. We should do it. Our own personalized reconnection list."

"Okay, may I propose the first bullet point? Let's not rob each other of our much-needed electronics…" My voice faded into a teasing smile.

"You just got me on board with your plan. Now you already seek to threaten it."

I shrugged. "I had to try."

She scooped up her wineglass and drank deeply. "We are not amused."

"You're a little amused. Admit it, you just like to torture me."

A smile tugged at her mouth and a knowing gaze. "Oh Mr. Drake, if you want torture, I know much better ways." She set her drink aside and turned back to me, her voice lowering with intensity. "For example… I could strap you down—"

I leaned forward on my elbows. "Now you have my attention—"

"—In front of a TV and play *The Last Jedi* on endless repeat."

I cringed, pressing a fist to the center of my chest. "Please, God, no. That's not the kind of torture I want from you."

Her sexy mouth twisted. "There's more where that came from."

I snickered. "You make it hurt so good."

Her brow arched. "Of course. *This is the way.*"

We laughed and finished our main course while we kept talking, tossing out ideas for the list—some serious, many joking.

"Please do not put *hold hands and stare into each other's eyes* on the list or I *will* gag," she said. Then she thanked our server, who cleared the plates and refilled our water glasses.

Once dessert was served—a rich salted caramel panna cotta encased by a chocolate sphere painted gold and garnished with marshmallow creme—our server bid us farewell. Before doing so, she indicated the location of an emergency services button and satellite phone should we need anything urgently. But otherwise, we were on our own and miles from any other human beings for the night.

"All joking aside," Emilia said as she considered the remains of her dessert after claiming she was too full for any more. "I honestly think a list that we come up with together is a really good idea. We should maybe have a little routine, or if you will, a ritual, something we do when you get back from being away on a work trip. Even if it's a simple as unplugging and watching movies in the theater room or going for a long walk and talking. Mindfulness. Making sure we are both present. And I'm not pointing fingers at you and the phone thing. You already know how I feel about that. I admit I do it, too—bury myself in my study materials instead of taking time out for a simple conversation or whatever."

I reached across the table and took her hand. "I'm not going to get cocky or complacent, but I think we have the beginnings of an amazing plan. Complacency is the enemy. We'll make a pact to keep working at this, okay?"

Her smile widened and she reached up to take my other hand across the table. Our eyes met and we sat there quietly staring at each other and holding hands.

Suddenly she jerked back. "Holy shit are we actually doing it spontaneously? Holding hands and staring into each other's eyes?"

I couldn't help it. The look of mock horror in her eyes made me laugh even harder.

"So enough of that... on to the good stuff! Anniversary presents." She rubbed her hands together. She pulled out the bag we'd brought with us and set two wrapped gifts on the table.

"I'm not sure we can do this every year because I gotta tell you that my creativity was taxed to the limit trying to figure out what I could possibly get for a billionaire that he couldn't just get for himself." I arched a brow and she held up a hand as if to stave off whatever pervy comment was about to come out of my mouth. "Besides sexual stuff."

She waved her hand. "You go first. I've been so excited for you to open it I almost gave it to you early."

"Well, now I'm intrigued, though it's a little too small to be hot lingerie for you to model for me later. Unless it's extra-skimpy."

As she shook her head, rolled her eyes, and otherwise feigned annoyance at my sexual innuendos, I picked it up, pretended to shake it.

"Just open it already!" she growled, and I laughed.

When I did, I pulled out a thick piece of card stock. It showed a rough sketch with a bold signature off to the side. It was by no means finished, and I tilted my head to the side, studying it, at first thinking it was maybe something William had started.

The scene, however, looked familiar. Two figures sitting across the table from each other. One of them held a gun under the table, pointed at the other. No, not a gun. A blaster...

Suddenly my level of excitement leapt. The signature in bold black sharpie leant it some authenticity.

"Is this...?"

"An original production sketch of Han Solo and Greedo in the Cantina from *A New Hope*. To commemorate the very serious discussion we had that night together in Amsterdam. Remember?"

I laughed. "Of course I do. This is amazing. And is this signature—from the man himself?"

She beamed, nodding proudly, quite pleased with herself. I didn't blame her. This was a major coup. "This isn't proof that Han shot first—a point I know is near and dear to your heart. Close enough, I guess?"

I stood from the table and ducked around it to land a peck on her lips. "I love it. This is awesome. Thank you. It's getting framed and put in my office immediately."

Then I nudged a small box toward her, a small white box tied with a red ribbon. "Time for you to open your gift."

# CHAPTER 34
## MIA

I WAS FEELING VERY PLEASED WITH MYSELF. AUTHENTIC memorabilia from the original trilogy was very hard to come by, even when you had the means to purchase it. And even though this had been paid for out of our joint bank account, I'd worked hard for this sucker. It had required hours of diligent research to track down. So when I made that purchase, I actually experienced a rush that must be what the thrill of the hunt is like.

And now, seeing his reaction, I was even more pleased.

He also had a self-satisfied smile on his face when he pushed the box with the prominent Cartier ribbon around it toward me.

Biting my lip, I pulled the bow and opened the box. Inside was a single bangle in rose gold. Simple, classy. Lovely. I wasn't big on showy jewelry but this was just my style. Understated.

I began to pull it out of the box to slip it on my wrist when a small object fell out with the bangle. It looked like a teeny screwdriver.

My brows raised. "What's this? In case I need to fix it?"

A mysterious smile played about Adam's mouth. Hmmm. He was up to something. He held out his hand. "Give it to me and I'll show you."

I handed him the miniature screwdriver and he pointed to the bangle, so I passed him that as well. It was thin and delicate, and now that I noticed it, four small diamonds and what looked like screws inscribed on the outside. I frowned, tilting my head to study it before realizing that Adam had taken the tiny screwdriver and was actually using it on one of the screw-like fastenings.

He held up one half of the circlet and showed me the engraving inside. *EKS + AD = Nat 20* and then our wedding date engraved inside. In spite of the fact that I so wasn't an ooey gooey sentimental and he knew it damn well, tears immediately sprang to my eyes so that I couldn't see anything through the blurriness.

He'd written that exact same thing on a padlock and affixed it at the top of the Eiffel Tower when we'd visited Paris. We'd been on shaky ground then. I was still recovering from cancer. Everything had seemed so fragile, uncertain. As far as I knew, that lock was still hanging there, in the middle of Paris. A statement to our love.

A sudden lump formed in my throat thinking of all the things we'd been through. The good, the amazing, and also the very sad. But in spite of it all, we'd fought, and we'd won. And we were a Natural 20—that magical gamer term from the roll of a dice, the ultimate geek symbol of winning.

Tonight, we'd made the decision to never get complacent in our relationship. But I held the enduring belief that if we'd survived such tough times already, we were meant to last the duration.

I blinked, pulled from those thoughts by the cold touch of metal against my wrist. One of his large, strong hands was wrapped around mine, holding it still. His thumb stroked the thin, sensitive skin there and I shivered. In his other hand, Adam turned the screwdriver to tighten the screw holding the bracelet together around my wrist.

"Nat 20…" I smiled. "Why not just say *we pwn?*"

"We do pwn. We are the ultimate gamer couple, after all."

I laughed. Another joke between us using that popular gaming slang that meant utterly defeating the opposition.

Adam tapped the metal band on my wrist. "I picked this out for the symbolism."

I sucked in a quick breath, taken with the erotic gesture of this moment of his holding me here, his wedding ring gleaming in the low light on the hand that held my arm steady. The act of him fixing it onto me. I swallowed, aware of everywhere I could feel my own heartbeat—in my throat, all through my body.

"This is a love bracelet," he said quietly. "It locks onto your arm with the screwdriver and screws," Adam explained.

"Subtle symbolism there." I examined it on my wrist once he'd finished. It was elegant, gorgeous. He still held my wrist tightly in his hand and I looked up, meeting his gaze, finding it hard to breathe. When I spoke, even I could hear the breathiness in my own voice. "Is this a socially acceptable handcuff? Are you handcuffing me?" I arched a brow.

He brought my hand to his lips and kissed my palm and the inside of my wrist without taking his eyes from mine. "You're getting me hard just talking about it."

I bit my lip. "I guess I don't need to bother changing into the little something I brought with me, then?"

His eyes smoldered into mine, and he shifted in his chair. "Yes, I think you definitely *do* need to bother."

In minutes, I emerged from the bathroom into the stylish, candlelit bedroom wearing the now infamous Agent

Provocateur lingerie I'd originally procured for our wedding night. With the shimmering fine chains and little gold medallions hanging from a barely-there framework, it covered hardly anything at all. This was our modern take on the chain mail bikinis I'd repeatedly teased him about all those years ago.

What had once been my big pet peeve about Dragon Epoch had become our sexy little in-joke.

"Oh damn." His eyes lit up. "I was wondering if I'd ever get to see that again. Hello, my old friend."

With a cheeky grin, I held out my arms and spun slowly for him. "You like?"

"Come here and I'll show you exactly how much I like it."

Our bedroom for the night was dominated by a lovely canopied and curtained four poster bed in dark, heavy wood. The huge picture window looked out across an empty field towards the mountains. Adam stood near that window and had been looking out of it when I'd entered. His jacket and tie had been shed, his shirt partially unbuttoned.

When I came within arm's reach, he pulled me against him and our mouths met in fiery union. He tasted like chocolate and red wine and smelled that salty ocean smell that was his scent alone.

My body came alive the moment his tongue slid into my mouth, and we were both breathing heavily seconds after that. But he broke away, surprisingly, to point out the window. "Look. There was a small chance we might be able to see something tonight..."

I turned in his arms, my back to his front, and he settled me there to lean against him. Up along the crest of the mountains against the sky, there was a faint green glow. "Is that...?"

"Aurora Borealis. Yup."

"Wow." I rested my head against his shoulder and his arms tightened around me. I watched the dim lights for a long moment, enjoying the electric sensation of his mouth on my neck at the juncture of my shoulder. My entire body heated, and I felt heavy, tense, my nipples and my core awakening.

"Happy New Year, Mrs. Drake," he whispered as he made his way up my neck to my ear, his hands roaming my body freely, sliding up my hips, my waist, to cup my breasts through the lingerie. The metallic discs pressed against my erect nipples, creating an explosion of sensation.

I let out a long moan, and he pressed himself closer, his erection prodding into my backside. I reached up behind me and hooked my arms around his neck to hold him there.

Inside, all sensation was molten, taut, each touch, each kiss felt across the entire surface of my skin. I turned in his arms, and between frantic kisses, I unbuttoned that crisp white shirt. I needed to feel his skin against mine.

"Happy anniversary, Mr. Drake," I breathed.

He'd turned a screw and locked the gift bracelet onto my arm but in truth, the lock that held me captive to him was one that couldn't be seen—couldn't be freed. His key and my lock, combined together sealed a love and the palpable chemistry between us into something no mechanism could reverse.

Soon enough, I had his clothes off. As slowly as I could manage, I sank to my knees in front of him. His breathing stuttered. Without hesitation, I took his cock into my mouth. The breath hissed completely out of him, his stance going rigid, eyes squeezing closed. Always my favorite part. I loved watching

Adam struggle to maintain control. while inevitably having it slip through his fingers. I loved being the one to cause it.

My mouth slid down his shaft, taking him deeper, and my reward came quickly—the growl deep in his throat. I felt it everywhere, from the prickling of my scalp, the frissons all over my skin, the molten heat between my legs.

He threaded his hands through my hair, holding my head still, even as I'd sought to quicken my pace. I struggled against his hold, but he pulled away from me, and with one gruff, swift gesture, he picked me up, took two steps, and tossed me roughly on the bed.

I stared up at him, shocked and momentarily breathless. Dark eyes drilled into mine, arms taught, hands clenched. "I need to fuck you, damn it. I can't wait another second."

I licked my lips, smiled, and then spread myself out deliberately for him without saying a word, stretching my arms above my head to touch the headboard, opening my legs. I waited.

His eyes scoured me from head to toe, scorching the flesh wherever they roamed. "I am the luckiest man on the planet, and I'm not even a little bit sorry about it."

"Come here," I echoed his words to him.

He held up a finger and disappeared into the other room. I lay back and stared up at the ceiling, idly fiddling with the thin bangle bracelet. The image of him locking it on me caused a surge of arousal. *Maybe we should try handcuffs sometime...*

Adam had been gone for a while...

I mean, longer than it should have taken for him to grab a handful of the little foil packets from the bag we'd brought with us and get back here.

*What the...?*

I propped my self up on my elbows and called into the next room. This wasn't a big cabin, after all. "What's the holdup?"

A second later, he appeared in the doorway in all of his naked glory. Mmmm. My husband was so gorgeous. Especially when he was naked. But the stricken look on his face? A little worrying.

"What's wrong?"

"I can't find the condoms."

"Did you look in the pockets? That bag has a lot of pockets."

He sighed, running a hand through his hair and approaching the bed. "Yes. I checked the pockets."

"There's an inside pocket that's zipped closed. Did you check that?"

"Yes. I said I checked all the pockets."

"Could it be—"

"I dumped the entire bag on the floor and looked through everything, Emilia. There are no condoms."

"Well... shit. I'm sorry I thought I threw some in there. Or maybe I was just assuming you would? It was such a crazy day."

He sighed. "I guess I did the same thing. It's nobody's fault."

I flopped back on the bed and he sat down beside me. I reached out and grabbed his hand, lacing my fingers with his. As a survivor of hormone-dependent breast cancer, I was banned for life from using any sort of hormonal birth control. That left us only two options—barrier methods or a non-hormonal IUD I'd been reluctant to choose. I wasn't comfortable with that option because of the level of invasiveness or possible complications it might pose.

Adam had never said a word about my decision—nor would he ever be the sort of man to pressure me to use an option I wasn't comfortable with. We'd done well with condoms as our option of choice.

I curled my fingers around his and tugged him toward me. "We don't need them. We can do other stuff just as fun."

He moved with my tug to lie down beside me. "That sounds interesting." He was smiling, but I detected a slight tinge of frustration. One hand slid under the metallic discs of the lingerie to rest on my belly.

We kissed, long and slow our hands finding the familiar places we knew the other liked to be touched. Skin warmed against skin. We kissed and touched and moved. And soon the chain mail bikini was history, a shimmery puddle on the floor. And our passion was reigniting that fire that had never truly gone out. Just paused.

My eyes fluttered closed, and I couldn't resist the pull and ache of how much I wanted him inside me. How much I wanted to feel his weight on top of me. I threaded a leg through his. And in between kisses, I dribbled out the idea that was forming in my head.

"You know…" Kiss. "We could always…" Kiss. "Just take this as…" More kisses. "A sign."

"A sign for what?" he breathed.

"A sign that maybe we could just be…" One long, especially passionate kiss with tongue and teeth. "Spontaneous."

"How?"

His mouth on my earlobe, my neck, my jaw. His hand between my legs, gently rubbing. Lightning behind my closed lids. "Let's just have sex without a condom and…see what happens."

He stilled.

One heartbeat. Two. He seemed to remember himself and his hand twitched just a little bit.

"You mean…?"

I turned my head to look into his face. "Why not?"

My hands were on him, moving across his flat, hard stomach, those bumpy abs I loved so much. I gripped him in my fist, sliding my palm along his length. His lids fell, and he sucked in a shaking breath. "You aren't fighting fair."

"I'm not fighting. I just want you inside me."

"Fuck, I want to be inside you."

My mouth slid across his chest, took in a nipple and teased it gently with the edge of my teeth. His fingers sifted my hair, pulling at it. "You are a witch, a temptress."

"Nope, just a woman who wants her husband to fuck her—hard."

In seconds he had me flipped on my back, and he was wedging himself between my legs, moving over me like a thunderstorm, wreaking havoc on my senses, with his hands, his mouth. His cock pushed against my entrance.

He shoved himself into me so quickly and hard that I cried out. But he didn't seem to notice, already driving himself into me with violent crashes, needy, hungry—as starving as I felt.

"Fuuuuck you feel so good. Oh my god, Emilia," he groaned against my neck. His length and girth inside of me, hard and ungiving,

I threw my head back, feeling that familiar rise toward orgasm, the pleasure seizing me by the throat and dragging me along with it. Behind my closed lids, I saw stars flare in conjunction with the swivel of his hips grinding against mine. I clamped onto his lower back, and ground my hips in answer—a call and response.

"Harder. Fuck me harder," I rasped against his neck, and then as if to punctuate my please, I sank my teeth into his neck. He grabbed my wrists and pinned them on either side of my head and leaned up on them, hovering over me to gain leverage. When I looked into his eyes, it was like seeing the eyes of a starving wolf staring into the face of his prey.

Our eyes met in that moment, and I couldn't breathe from the intensity of our connection. Suddenly my body arched against his, the orgasm overtaking me with a sudden force I hadn't expected. He slammed against me and explosions of pleasure erupted from my core, spreading in shockwaves all over my body.

"Adam, oh, oh *yes*."

It kept going. And I was stunned, breathless and shivering beneath him as he continued his relentless pace, releasing my wrists and pushing up on his arms until—

He slipped out of me, and after a beat, he stiffened. He came against my thigh. With a rough growl, he let out a long breath of release.

I blinked, trying to examine this feeling. Sure, it had been impulse to ask him. We hadn't discussed this since right before our wedding. But somehow in this moment, the possibility had seemed so right, and even... exhilarating.

*I wanted this...* it felt like time.

And though I wasn't terribly surprised that Adam had pulled out, I had to admit that I was disappointed.

We didn't talk for a long time, only held each other in the dark, our sweaty bodies turning chilly. When he finally rolled off of me, instead of leaving the room immediately to avoid the impending discussion, like he might have done in our earlier days, he turned to me instead.

"I'm sorry," he rasped.

I turned to him, putting a palm against his whiskery cheek. "Why on earth are you apologizing to the women you just made come so hard she saw stars?"

He took in a deep breath and released it again, his breath still faster than normal. And he watched me, examined every inch of my face. "I know what you were asking."

I nodded. "Of course you did. You know how babies are made."

He swallowed, then shook his head. "I can't—I mean I couldn't. I can't be spontaneous with this. There's just so much—"

"Shhh." I pressed my thumb to his lips and he automatically kissed it. "It's okay. I'm not mad. It *was* spontaneous. But I understand. To ask you do make this decision on a lark because you wanted sex was asking you to be something you can't be. I know the man I married. I know you don't work that way."

He lowered his head and kissed my temple, the tops of my eyes through my closed lids. "I love you so much."

"I know." I laughed, giving that old Han Solo response we used to enjoy exchanging back in the day. I rested in the nook of his arm, my cheek pressed to his chest and I couldn't shake this feeling... as if making that impulsive suggestion had opened a Pandora's box of yearning desire within me.

I kissed his chest. "Adam?"

"Yes?"

"I really do want to have your baby. And, to me, it feels like we're ready."

He blew out a breath. "Emilia. The idea crossed your mind fifteen minutes ago. How can you—"

"It was a sudden suggestion but it's been at the back of my mind for years, you know? Since our loss… I really want us to try again."

"But the risk—"

I met his gaze, stared deeply into his eyes. "I promise you I will always be honest with you. And yes, there is a risk. But there's always a risk. For everyone. It might not be cancer or whatever. But risk is always there. It's *life*, Adam. And I want to live it. I want a family with you." I took his hand and placed the flat of it against my stomach. "I want to feel your child growing here. Or if that's not possible, to build a family in another way. But I want us to be parents because I think we'd be pretty fucking amazing at it."

Another long silence where he was impossibly still, like a statue. Then he brushed my cheek with the back of his fingers. "Let's sit down and have a serious conversation about it when we get home."

I bit my lip. Was he stalling again? But how to bring that up without a confrontation?

He seemed to read those thoughts in my eyes.

"I'm not putting this off. We'll have that discussion, I promise you. You can put it on the calendar. But you know me. I need research, data, medical opinions. Best practices—"

I bust out laughing. "Oh, I think we have the 'best practices' part down quite well already."

For the first time since I'd proposed us having unprotected sex tonight, he laughed, too. "We do that part incredibly well, that's true."

I placed my hands on either side of his head and stared into those fathomless dark eyes. So serious. So responsible. So intent on keeping me absolutely safe from any sort of harm. "I love you, husband."

He kissed me with a smile on his face, then nuzzled my neck in a spot he knew was ticklish. "I love you, Emilia. Always."

"Mm. We're a Nat 20, never forget it."

"Absolutely," he breathed.

Not long later, we nestled together under the covers. He wrapped himself around me and I listened to him drift off into a peaceful sleep, his breath coming steady and calm. I stared out the window at the glowing mountain scape, basking in the quiet and secure feelings of safety and happiness in my husband's arms.

We'd been through so much. I completely understood where his fears came from. But fears could be faced—and hopefully, overcome.

As for me, well, I could only feel excitement for what lay ahead of us.

Because easy or hard, we'd pwn it all. And we'd do it together.

Brenna Aubrey is a USA TODAY Bestselling Author of contemporary romance stories that center on geek culture. Her debut novel, At Any Price, is currently free on all platforms.

She has always sought comfort in good books and the long, involved stories she weaves in her head. Brenna is a city girl with a nature-lover's heart. She therefore finds herself out in green open spaces any chance she can get. She's also a mom, teacher, geek girl, Francophile, unabashed video-game addict & eBook hoarder.

She currently resides on the west coast with her husband, two children, two adorable golden retriever pups, a bird and some fish.

More information available at www.BrennaAubrey.net

To sign up for Brenna's email list for release updates, please copy & paste this link into your browser:
http://BrennaAubrey.net/newsletter-signup/

Want to discuss the Gaming The System series with other avid readers? Brenna's reader discussion and social group is located on Facebook
https://www.facebook.com/groups/BrennaAubreyBookGroup/